*When Violet helped some runaway slaves escape, she knew she was placing her own freedom at risk.*

Violet was in the storeroom looking over some bolts of fabric when Louise entered, her face pale.

"Violet," she whispered, leaning forward over a wooden packing crate, "There are some deputies here to speak with you."

Violet froze. The back of her neck broke into a cold sweat as she stood holding a bolt of Jersey cloth.

"Are you in some kind of trouble?" Louise asked.

"Yes ma'am." Violet's voice matched the lifeless expression in her eyes. "I expect that I am."

**KATE BLACKWELL** is a former kindergarten teacher who now stays home to pursue her lifelong dream of writing novels.

**Other Books by Kate Blackwell**

HP20—Shores of Promise

# Shores of Deliverance

*Kate Blackwell*

A sequel to **Shores of Promise**

*Heartsong Presents*

*This book is dedicated to Buddy Blackwell, my husband and best friend, who patiently does the page numbering, disc back-ups, and other things that his computer-illiterate wife cannot fathom.*

*Special thanks to Gilbert Morris, my writing mentor, for sharing so much of his knowledge, wisdom, and enthusiasm.*

ISBN 1-55748-437-6

**SHORES OF DELIVERANCE**

# *one*

Violet Bowman had always been a light sleeper, but it took a few seconds for her to realize that the soft, insistent knocking was not part of a dream. That awareness jolted her awake.

"Who's there?" she called out into the blackness of her room, aiming her voice in the direction of the door.

The knocking stopped, but there was no answer. Clutching her sheet to her neck, she could hear nothing but the pulse pounding in her ears. Then again, the knocking sounded.

"Who's there!" she called impatiently.

"It's me. Willis!" came back the muffled reply.

Quickly, Violet slipped out of bed. She felt for her flannel wrapper hanging on the iron bedstead and put it on over her nightgown. Hurrying to the door, she fumbled with the latch. "What is—"

She let out a small cry and jumped back as the heavy pine door was pushed toward her.

"I'm sorry to scare you like that, Miss Violet," a man whispered, stepping from the dark hallway into her even darker room. She recognized Willis's voice.

"You come in too," he said to two dark forms outside the door. "Hurry!"

Her heart racing, Violet felt her way over to her dresser and lit a candle. Turning, she caught in its light the lined face of Willis Simmons, a former slave like herself and a deacon at Mount Zion Baptist Church. With him were a young black man and woman, both staring wide-eyed at her.

"This here's Caleb and Opal Martin," Willis said, motioning toward the couple. "They stowed away on a freighter from Jacksonville a couple weeks ago. I been keepin' them at my place, but I just got word that some agents are in my part of town lookin' and asking questions."

Violet felt a stab of fear for her elderly friend. Slave agents were often ruthless men hired by planters to hunt down runaways in the free states and territories, under the authority of the Federal Fugitive Slave Law of 1793.

Violet recalled how four years earlier the United States Supreme Court had given its blessing to these bounty hunters with its 1842 decision in the Prigg case. It forbade any state interference with the bounty hunters' performance of their duties.

Advertisements frequently ran in the *Gazetteer* offering rewards for information leading to the recapture of certain slaves. Boston was known to be a temporary haven for runaways making their way to Canada.

"Do they know you've been hiding these two?"

Willis shook his graying head. "I don't think so. Not yet. But too many people knows about it. It's hard to keep the grandchildren from talkin' about what goes on at home. They just too young to understand, and they never knowed about bein' a slave." A look of anguish covered his face. "I should'a sent them on up to Maine last Monday when Mr. Phelps offered his wagon."

"That wasn't your fault, Mr. Willis." Opal spoke from beside her husband. "You was worried about me." Turning bashful eyes to Violet, she said quietly, "I lost my baby."

Violet's heart went out to the young woman, who appeared to be not much more than a child herself. "I'm sorry," she whispered.

Silence hung over them as they stood in the circle of candlelight. Finally, Willis cleared his throat. "I hate like everything to get you involved in all this, Miss Violet, but they needs a place to stay tonight."

"Tonight?"

"I think just tonight—maybe tomorrow night, too. I ain't gone to lie to you. It might be a whole week 'fore we can get them out of town.

The heaviness in the man's voice matched the heaviness in Violet's soul. Willis was asking her to risk going to jail if the Martins were captured.

She had no qualms about disobeying the law against harboring runaway slaves. Violet believed Christians should obey the law, but not when it conflicted with God's higher laws. She likened the abolitionists to the Hebrew midwives in Moses' time, who refused to obey Pharaoh's orders to kill newborn male babies of the Hebrew slaves.

So far, though, the only thing she'd been asked to sacrifice toward this principal was a portion of her salary, after her tithe. The New England Freedom Association, founded in Boston a few years earlier, was always in urgent need of funds for aiding fugitives on their journeys to freedom.

Now Violet was being asked to risk her position as a seamstress in the dress shop below her room, not to mention her freedom. She could only make one choice.

"All right," she said.

## two

"How would you like to go to England next month?" David Adams asked his wife, Sarah, as they sat together on the front porch of their Charleston home.

The fluid motion of Sarah's arm came to a halt as she held her fan poised in mid-air. She searched her husband's face for any sign of teasing. "Did you say England?"

David looked anxious. "Bristol, mainly, and a few other stops. Matthew asked today if I would see to our accounts there." He ran a hand through his close-cropped blond hair. "I don't want to pressure you to go if you're not ready to travel, but I hate like everything the thought of going without you."

Bristol! Sarah let out the breath she'd been holding since David had spoken the name of the town where she'd spent her first sixteen years. So many painful memories. *How could I consider going back?*

After all, her life was almost perfect. Her husband, David, was her best friend, and little Eileen, at eighteen months, was a constant source of joy. *The only time I was happy in Bristol,* Sarah mused, *was when I was with my mother—and that didn't last long enough.*

The thought of her mother brought a sudden pang to Sarah's heart. *Eileen will never know how beautiful her grandmother was. I don't even have a picture to show her.*

Sarah's mother, Ruth Brown, had died of pneumonia from working in a textile mill when Sarah was fourteen years old. Mrs. Gerty, the woman whom Sarah had been working for, hadn't allowed the young girl time off to attend the funeral, if indeed there had been one.

"Sarah?" David's soft voice brought her back to the present. "What are you thinking about?"

"My mother." The compassion on her husband's face brought tears to Sarah's brown eyes. "I shouldn't feel so sad because I've been so blessed with you and the baby, but—"

"You miss her."

A lump at the back of her throat, Sarah could only nod.

David took her hand and rested it against his smooth-shaven cheek. "I would like to have known her."

She had to smile in spite of her tears, for his words were typical David. Not only did her husband have a gift for saying the right thing, but he was sincere, as well. He would have treated her mother like he treated his own, with tenderness and respect.

"The only thing is," she said, remembering a promise she'd made some time ago, "I wrote Violet that we'd be taking that trip to Boston before Christmas. I haven't seen her in so long, and I know she'd love to see Eileen."

"It may work out after all," said David, his face hopeful. "We'd have to take a brig to Boston and meet a clipper ship for the crossing. We could leave a day or two early, and you could visit with Violet."

"I could?"

"Why not? I'd like to meet the woman who led my wife to Christ. She must be something."

Sarah nodded. "She is." A picture of her friend's intelligent dark eyes and ready smile came to mind. It would be so good to see her again!

Two years after she'd emigrated to the United States, eighteen-year-old Sarah had been hired by Jonathan Bowman, the owner of a South Carolina rice plantation, to be a companion to his ailing mother. That's when she'd met Violet, a house slave her own age.

Sarah's heart had been filled with an intense longing for something she couldn't identify. After much soul-searching, she'd realized that the answer to her yearning might be found in a handwritten notebook of Scripture that she had received from a young man she'd met during her journey to America.

When the illiterate Sarah discovered that Violet could read, she begged the slave girl to give her secret lessons. Reading Scripture with Violet, Sarah came to understand the way of salvation provided to her by God through His Son, Jesus Christ.

Sarah grew to love her friend so much that when Jonathan Bowman, whom she did not love, offered to free Violet up North in exchange for Sarah's hand in marriage, she'd agreed.

Sarah realized again that her husband had spoken. "What did you say?" she asked sheepishly.

"I said, 'I hope Willie Mae fixes elephant stew again for supper.'" answered David with a wink. "And you nodded your head."

"I'm sorry. I'm doing it again."

David kissed the tips of her fingers. "You don't have to apologize. I've given you a lot to think about. This trip is a big decision."

"Actually, I was thinking about Violet—and you. I still have that book you gave me back then." Sarah had never imagined that the man who had given her the book of handwritten Scripture would someday be her husband.

David had been a virtual stranger then, an American returning from a business trip in England and engaged to be married. He didn't marry, though, and Sarah came across him again at church three years later, after her first husband, Jonathan, had died from malaria.

"I know," David was saying, obviously pleased that the leather-bound book still meant so much to her. "I've seen it in the cedar chest."

The tired tinkling of harness chains in the evening dimness drew their attention to Chance Street which fronted their property. Still holding hands, David and Sarah watched a long-suffering gray mule pull a wagon of feed sacks toward the Ashley River.

As the mule disappeared from sight, the new house-maid, Elsa, opened the front screened door and peered out at them. "Miss Willie Mae says that supper's ready," she drawled softly before disappearing.

"Well, let's go have at that elephant stew," said David, stretching his legs.

Sarah took his proffered hand and rose to her feet. "I want to go," she told him on their way to the front door.

He looked at her sideways. "To supper?"

"To Boston—and to England."


"Mrs. Fairchild was impressed with that yellow sprigged muslin you made for her," Louise Johnson said to Violet, watching her guide a pair of scissors around a length of sea-green sateen.

The women were in the sewing room directly behind Louise's dress shop, a busy establishment on Chimes Street in downtown Boston. In the four years since Violet had applied for a job at the shop, she'd worked her way up to head seamstress, supervising two other seamstresses and a young apprentice.

Glancing up from her work, Violet grinned at her employer. "The lady was convinced that she was too heavy to wear anything but dark colors. I'm glad she changed her mind."

"Well, you have a way of talking people into doing things—just like you talked me into hiring you."

Violet's cheeks grew warm as she thought of the two runaway slaves in her room. *I have a way of getting talked into doing things, too.* She didn't like deceiving Louise. The red-haired woman sympathized with the abolitionists and subscribed to William Lloyd Garrison's anti-slavery newspaper, the *Liberator*. But how Louise would feel about harboring fugitives, Violet didn't know, and she couldn't afford to ask at the moment.

Anyway, her worries would be over soon. Caleb and Opal had been hidden away in her upstairs room for three days, and Willis had sent word that morning that he'd found a way to get the couple out of Boston.

One week later, Violet was in the storeroom looking over some bolts of fabric when Louise entered, her face pale.

"Violet," she whispered, leaning forward over a wooden packing crate. "There are some deputies here to speak with you."

Violet froze. The back of her neck broke into a cold sweat as she stood holding a bolt of Jersey cloth.

"Are you in some kind of trouble?" Louise asked.

"Yes ma'am." Violet's voice matched the lifeless expression in her eyes. "I expect that I am."

Sarah's brown eyes were red and swollen when she met David in the front parlor Monday evening.

"What's wrong, dear?" he asked as soon as he'd hung up his hat. He shot a glance at the stairway leading to the bedrooms and nursery. "Is the baby sick?"

She shook her head. "This came today." After handing him a creased sheet of paper, she slumped into the closest armchair.

No lantern had been lit, so David brought the paper over to a front window and caught the rays of the setting sun. Holding the letter in front of him, he read:

> *Dear Mrs. Adams,*
>
> *I thought you should know that Violet was arrested four days ago for hiding some runaway slaves. The slaves, a young married couple, safely left the city several days before her arrest, but somehow the agents traced their escape route to her.*
>
> *Her trial is in three weeks. I have retained an attorney with some experience with these cases, but I fear Violet will be sent to prison. The judge assigned to her trial is reputed to be hostile to people who harbor fugitives.*
>
> *I remember meeting you three years ago when you came to visit Violet, and I apologize for waiting these four days to think about writing you. I found your address on the front leaf of her Bible when she asked me to bring it to her in jail.*
>
> *Please keep her in your prayers. I shall write you after the trial and tell you the verdict.*
> *Sincerely,*
> *Louise Johnson*

David lowered the letter. "We've got to help her."

"How?" asked Sarah in a whisper. Her throat was sore from weeping.

"This was sent two weeks ago," he said. "That means her trial is in seven days." Setting the letter on a lamp table, David walked to where his wife sat and knelt down on one knee. "There's some paperwork I've got to finish before our trip. If I rush it, I can have it finished by Friday. That's two days before we planned to leave for Boston."

Sarah's head jerked up. "You mean it? Do you think we could visit her in jail?"

David nodded, but his face was serious. "I don't want to see you distressed any more than you already are, but I don't like the tone of that letter. There's a lot of anger down here toward the abolitionists, and it looks like the owner of those two slaves is out to make an example of Violet."

Wiping her eyes with her handkerchief, Sarah asked, "What can we do?"

"I wish we had more time. Then I could find out where this owner lives and offer to reimburse him for the two slaves."

"Won't he be in Boston?"

"Not likely. The letter says that slave agents arrested her. They have the power to demand prosecution, even in free states like Massachusetts, but they'd have no authority to accept money from me and drop the charges. By the time they could contact their employer and get his answer, the trial would be over."

"Poor Violet," murmured Sarah. "Her faith is so strong, but I wonder if she's afraid."

Still kneeling at his wife's side, David said, "We'll pray that God takes care of her." He shook his head. "I wish now that I'd turned down this trip to England. It's too late to back out."

The next morning, sixteen-year-old Elsa had just walked into the parlor with a handful of clean dust rags when she realized Sarah was sitting on the sofa. Baby Eileen was sleeping beside her, her head resting on her mother's lap.

"I'm sorry, ma'am," Elsa whispered, backing toward the door.

Sarah motioned for her to come nearer. "I need to talk with you." The baby stirred, then nestled her curly head deeper into the space between her mother's side and the padded arm of the sofa.

"She'll be waking up soon anyway," said Sarah. She motioned toward the space beside her on the sofa. "Come sit with us."

Elsa quickly complied, setting the dust rags in her lap. "Ma'am?"

She tried to figure out what wrong she'd committed, a habit ingrained in her when she was a ten-year-old maid in the Clarks' household. The fact that Sarah and David had been so kind to her since she'd been employed by them two weeks earlier made matters worse. Elsa knew that one day she'd make a mistake big enough for them to realize how stupid she was. Then they'd scream at her like Mrs. Clark, maybe even slap her!

"I want to tell you that I appreciate the job you're doing," Sarah was saying while she patted the baby's back. "Sometimes I think you work too hard."

Elsa's mouth fell open. "You do?"

"Very much." Sarah smiled at her. "You know, I didn't want to hire a maid."

*I knew it. I'm about to get fired!* Elsa thought. *She's*

*tryin' to keep from hurting my feelings about it.*

"See, I've been a maid for most of my life," Sarah told her. "And I thought I could handle the housework myself, especially with Willie Mae taking care of the cooking. My husband tried to convince me that I should have more servants, but I thought I wouldn't be comfortable living that way."

She shrugged her shoulders, then looked down at the baby in her lap. "This little sweetheart changed things. I tried to take care of everything myself for a long time, but finally my husband insisted." Giving Elsa a smile, Sarah said, "And so you came into our lives."

Elsa already knew that her mistress had been a maid. Willie Mae had told her that in the kitchen on her first day, with her face lit up as if she was saying something wonderful. The news had filled Elsa with dread, for she'd imagined that a former servant would be extremely demanding and fault-finding.

"I'm. . .glad you like my work," said Elsa, her cheeks flushed with pleasure. She paused, not sure what was expected of her.

"Is that all?" she managed to say.

Shaking her head, Sarah answered, "There's something else. Mr. Adams and I plan to leave for Boston Friday. Then we'll be going on to England." A shadow passed across her face. "While we're in Boston, I'll need someone to keep Eileen while my husband and I. . .visit a friend."

Elsa took in a quick breath. Boston? She'd never been on a ship, never been outside of Charleston in her whole life.

"Are you wantin' me to go to Boston?" she asked, hardly daring to hope that Sarah would say yes.

"Not only Boston. I think it would be nice to have you on the whole trip. I've never traveled with the baby. I think she'll do fine, but—"

"Oh, you won't have to worry a bit about Eileen!" Elsa assured her, her voice filled with excitement. "I'll tend to her every minute!"

Actually, she'd had no experience taking care of babies. The Clarks had employed nannies and governesses, and as a kitchen maid, Elsa had hardly been around the children. She determined that she would learn.

Sarah smiled. "Well, I do expect to spend most of the time with her myself. But I appreciate that you're willing to come. To tell you the truth, I wasn't sure what to do with you. I told Willie Mae of our plans before breakfast, and she's excited about having time off to visit her sister in Mobile—we're still going to pay her salary, of course.

"But you," she continued. "You don't have any family, do you?"

"No ma'am." Elsa lowered her eyes. "I had a daddy once, but I heard he was dead a few years ago."

"And your mother?"

"I don't remember her. My Aunt Hattie raised me until I was old enough to get a job. She died last year."

Sarah's face was sympathetic. "Do you miss her?"

"Yes, ma'am," answered Elsa, giving the expected response. *But that's not really true, she admitted to herself. She told me every day that I was trash, on account of my daddy.*

"We have a lot in common," said Sarah. "No parents except for our heavenly Father."

Eileen whimpered, held up her head, and looked around as if disoriented. Her curls, chestnut brown like her mother's, were slightly damp where she'd been lying on them.

"Hello, little girl," cooed Sarah, helping the baby crawl up into her lap. "Can you say 'hello' to Elsa?"

Her cheeks still rosy from sleep, Eileen pointed a chubby finger at the maid. Then she suddenly turned bashful and buried her head in her mother's chest.

Sarah laughed. "Turning shy, are you?" Giving Elsa an apologetic look, she said, "She's not used to being around you. I think you two will become best friends before too long."

Impulsively Elsa reached out to touch the baby's dimpled elbow. "I hope so, ma'am," she said wistfully. "I'd like that lots."

That night in her cellar room, Elsa brought out the trunk Sarah had insisted she use and packed the clothing she could do without before the trip. As she bent over an opened dresser drawer to take out a nightgown, her reflection in the mirror caught her eye. Straightening, she frowned at the image glowering back at her.

*Stupid and ugly,* she thought. She raked her fingers through her limp, wheat-colored hair. *It's a wonder anyone wants me around.* Tall and thin, Elsa had acquired the habit of walking with her shoulders slumped. Her mouth, too wide for her face, drew attention away from her sapphire blue eyes, her one mark of beauty.

She hadn't been able to believe her good fortune when the Adams had hired her. Mildred, the cook in the Clarks' house, had met Willie Mae at church and learned that the Adams were thinking about hiring a maid.

Mildred had been Elsa's only friend and had often expressed disgust at the way the Clarks and other servants treated the young maid. At Mildred's urging, Elsa had steeled herself to apply for the job before the Adams could put an advertisement in the *Courier*.

*And now I'm going to England!* Maybe there was something to what Miss Sarah had told her about having a heavenly Father, for it seemed lately that someone was indeed watching over her.

For three days, David put in long hours to prepare the documents necessary for his business abroad. Matthew Wesley, his employer and the owner of Charleston Shipping Management Company, lent him a hand several times, so by late Thursday the paperwork was completed.

"We can leave tomorrow morning like we planned," David announced when he arrived home after dark. His shoulders were sagging and his eyes had circles under them, but he enveloped Sarah in a hug.

"I'm afraid I'm still short," he mumbled into her ear. That was an old joke with them, for David stood only an inch or two taller than his wife. He yawned. "Are we packed for tomorrow?"

"All packed," said Sarah. "Willie Mae is holding supper warm for you."

"Please thank her for me, but I'm going to get some sleep." Giving her a kiss, he added, "I want to be rested for the battle we're heading into."

# three

Sarah tied the strings to her straw bonnet tighter as the carriage swayed down the uneven cobblestones of Court Street that Saturday morning. A muggy summer wind pressed against the woven fabric of her dress and stirred tendrils of hair that had escaped from their hairpins.

"Is that the courthouse?" she asked David beside her.

David nodded toward an imposing three-story building of red brick. "That's it. Violet should be upstairs somewhere.

Staring up at the rows of iron-barred windows, Sarah fought back tears. She had to be strong for her friend's sake. Crying could come later.

A stern-faced guard with heavy eyebrows led them down a hall lined with iron doors. Bars about an inch thick hung on a square opening cut into the top half of each door. The guard stopped at the last cell on the right and lifted the metal bolt, letting the bars swing to the side of the frame.

Sarah peered through the opening and saw Violet looking up from her canvas cot.

"Sarah?" she said wonderingly, coming to her feet just as the door swung open.

The sound of her friend's voice broke Sarah's resolve to not cry. She rushed into the cell and threw her arms around Violet.

"Here, here now," murmured the dark-skinned woman, patting Sarah's back. "Everything's going to be all right."

"We came to comfort you," cried Sarah, her voice

20

muffled by Violet's shoulder. "Here you are telling me everything's going to be all right!"

"Well it is," soothed Violet. "I've got a peace about this. Whatever happens, the Lord's got a purpose in it, and He's not going to make me go through it alone."

Stepping back, Sarah wiped her eyes with the back of her hand. "I want you to meet my husband," she said, sniffling.

"David." Violet offered a brown hand to the man who'd been standing in silence.

David clasped her hand with both of his. "I'm sorry I didn't get to meet you the last time we came to Boston—business kept me occupied that whole trip." He glanced around the eight-by-ten cell. "Are you being treated decently?"

"Yes," answered Violet. "I'm allowed to have visitors, and the meals are regular. It could be a lot worse."

*Prison will be a lot worse*, thought Sarah. She forced herself to smile. "You have many visitors?"

"Many. I can only see two at a time, but there are hundreds of people praying for me."

"Really?" David raised his eyebrows. "You mean an organized group of people?"

Nodding, Violet said, "The New England Anti-Slave Society has been holding meetings at Faneuil Hall almost every night since I was arrested." Glancing toward the guard standing outside the cell door, she lowered her voice. "It's hard to believe all those people care what happens to me, but I sure am glad to know it."

David considered her words. "Do you think we could attend these meetings?"

"I don't see why not," said Violet. "My trial's Monday,

so they'll be gathering there tonight and Sunday night after church. Be sure and look for Miss Louise Johnson, the lady I work for." Folding her arms, she turned back to Sarah. "That's enough about me. I want to hear all about little Eileen!"

Carriages and wagons lined the streets around Faneuil Hall, a brick, three-story building in Dock Square. Not long after David and Sarah found seats, the meeting hall on the first floor was packed with people of both races.

"I think I see Miss Johnson," Sarah said above the steady hum of voices. Rising a couple inches from the wooden pew, she pointed several rows ahead. "It's a good thing she has red hair and isn't wearing a hat."

"We'll have to catch her after the meeting," said David.

On the platform in front of the room were two men seated to the left of the pulpit, one black and the other white. A middle-aged white woman was standing behind the pulpit, attractively dressed in a high-collared chambray dress and a fashionable rolling brim straw hat. She called the meeting to order.

"That's Maria Weston Chapman," whispered the man seated next to David, in answer to his inquiry. "She's the editor of the *Liberty Bell*." David had heard of the annually published book during his travels. Anti-slavery essays, sermons, stories, and poems were featured, and its sales raised money for abolitionist causes.

"Reverend Milton Andrews will lead us in prayer," Mrs. Chapman was saying at the front. "Please rise."

The black man to her left walked to the pulpit. Clearing his throat, he prayed with a gentle humility for Violet, for those still in slavery, and for the slave owners.

When the last "amen" had echoed throughout the hall, the minister returned to his seat. Mrs. Chapman then introduced the evening's speaker, William Lloyd Garrison.

The balding, white man stood. He gave Mrs. Chapman a slight bow as he passed her on his way to the podium. Unimpressive in appearance, he strode confidently to the pulpit.

"Ladies and Gentlemen, Miss Bowman's trial is in two days," he said, getting down to business right away. Though he looked to be in his late thirties or early forties, his voice sounded decades older. "We have gathered here these past nights to make speeches and declare our indignation, and rightly so. But I suggest that no speech, no matter how eloquent, will free Miss Bowman. I suggest that it is time to decide upon an action and decide if we have the courage to take that action."

"Attack the court house!" yelled a voice from the audience. "We've got more than three hundred here. We can get her out of there!"

A husky white man who'd been seated on the front row jumped to his feet and turned to face the crowd. "No matter how many there are of us, we can't fight against iron bars and armed guards! They'll hide her away somewhere, and some of us will end up dead!"

"You call that courage?" came another voice from the audience, to the hoots and applause of several in the room.

"I call it being realistic!" the man boomed back before taking his seat.

Mr. Garrison held up his hands to quell the rumbles of agreement and dissent. "I agree with Mr. Sanders," he said. "Violence should be used only as a last resort. There is another way."

Several voices shouted out at once. "Tell us!"

"I think all of us who can should show our support for Miss Bowman by being present at her trial Monday morning."

"And then what?" came a woman's voice.

"That's all I can tell you now," said Mr. Garrison, speaking slowly and purposefully. "What's of utmost importance is to have as many of us as possible at the trial. We need to fill up that court room, even the halls!" He paused a few seconds for effect. "Then we need to keep our eyes and ears open!"

Above the voices rippling through the auditorium, someone yelled out, "Can't you tell us more than that?"

The man behind the pulpit gave a fatherly smile. "Need I remind you that even our Lord Jesus had a traitor in the midst of His friends? All I can say is please be at the trial Monday morning."

After the meeting was dismissed, David led Sarah through the crowd to find Violet's employer, Louise Johnson. She was gathering papers from the pew in which she'd sat, but looked up before they could speak to her.

"Mrs. Adams!" she exclaimed with a smile. "I spoke with Violet just before the meeting and she told me you'd be here. How good of you to come all the way to Boston!"

Sarah clasped the woman's gloved hand, then said, "This is my husband, David."

"I'm pleased to meet you, Miss Johnson." David shook the hand she offered. "I know Sarah appreciates how you've taken care of her friend."

Louise waved away his praise. "Violet would have done it for me, if our situations had been reversed."

"Is there anything we can do to help?" asked David.

"You've helped by being here. I was amazed at how much her spirits were lifted this afternoon. Will you be able to stay for the trial?"

Her face clouding, Sarah said, "We have to leave for England early Tuesday morning. Do you think the trial will be over by then?"

"Probably." Tilting her head, Louise studied David's face. "You're going to England?"

He looked miserable. "I wish we could postpone our trip, but we've sent letters ahead scheduling appointments, and it would hurt my employer if I didn't keep them."

Louise didn't seem to have heard, for she said, "Tuesday morning?"

"Yes," answered David.

"We plan to see Violet as soon as we get back to the States," Sarah told her. She bit her lip. "Wherever she'll be."

"What hotel are you staying in?" asked Louise, her expression still preoccupied.

David flashed his wife a puzzled glance. "Meribell Inn, on South Market Street."

The red-haired woman nodded. "Would you mind sitting here for a little while? I need to speak with some people."

"Not at all," answered David.

"Thank you." She started to walk off, then turned back to them. "By the way, do you remember what the guard looked like? The one who escorted you to see Violet?"

"Mean-looking," Sarah said without hesitation. "He had fierce black eyebrows and hardly spoke to us."

Louise grinned. "Excellent!"

Giving Sarah and David an appreciative smile, Louise hurried to the front of the room where seven people, including those who'd been on the platform, had their heads together.

"Do you suppose Elsa and Eileen are all right?" asked Sarah as she watched Miss Johnson join the group in front.

"I asked the steward to check on them occasionally," David reassured her.

"I'm so pleased at how well Elsa is—" Sarah cut herself off. "David, they're looking at us!"

"You're right. I wonder what she's telling them?"

They both sat in silence and watched the animated conversation taking place near the platform. Once in a while, someone from the small group would look in their direction. Mr. Garrison gave them a nod and a smile.

Thirty minutes later, Miss Johnson came back to David and Sarah. "I apologize for keeping you so long," she said.

"Miss Johnson, what is this all about?" asked David. "Is there something you need? We want to help if we can."

"Do you mean that?" The woman's face was serious.

"Of course."

"I'm glad to hear that. You can help Violet by not visiting her anymore."

"What?" Sarah sat up straight. "What do you mean?"

"I mean it would be better for her if you stayed away tomorrow."

"Now, Miss Johnson," began David, "my wife and Violet are as close as any two sisters. Tomorrow—"

"Is Sunday. Go to church somewhere—take a picnic on the Common. When evening comes, go back to your room and stay there."

David opened his mouth to speak, then closed it again. He watched the woman's face in front of him warily, wondering if she'd lost her mind.

"Do you understand my meaning?" Louise asked calmly.

The auditorium was empty—even the leaders who had gathered at the front were gone. In the quietness that enveloped them, it dawned on David that Miss Johnson was sending him a message with her eyes. Hesitating only for a second, he nodded. "I understand."

From her husband's side, Sarah took in a sharp breath. *Could she possibly be telling us that. . . .*

"What I need to know," Louise said evenly, "is, are you *positive* that you want to get involved with this?"

"Positive." David's face was grave. "We want to help Violet."

"Do you plan to stay in your room tomorrow night?"

"Yes. All night."

The woman was beaming at them. "You two are an answer to prayer."


Back at their fourth-floor hotel suite that night, David paced the floor while Sarah and Elsa played with the baby. Doubts assaulted him with fury. *Are they really going to arrange an escape? Was all that talk about needing everyone to attend the trial a diversion? That had to be it! After all, Mr. Garrison had hinted that traitors to the cause could be present.*

*What happens if they bring Violet here and we get caught? My family, what would happen to them?* He would insist that Sarah had nothing to do with the operation so that he alone would go to prison. Then what?

David stood at one of the suite's eight screened windows, allowing the night-cooled breeze to bathe his face. A soft hand slipped into his. He turned to see Sarah regarding him thoughtfully.

"You're a good man," she whispered.

All was silent, save the faint rustling of brocade curtains. David glanced over his shoulder to find everyone else gone.

"I asked Elsa to take the baby in her room to bathe her and dress her for bed," said Sarah. She smiled. "I was so worried that Eileen wouldn't want anyone beside me tending to her. After all, she hasn't been around Elsa much."

Had there really been a time when all they'd had to worry about was if the baby would take to her sitter? A hundred years ago, thought David.

"I'm not a good man," he told her.

"Why do you say that?" she asked, looking surprised.

"Because right now I'm fighting the urge to take you and Eileen back to Charleston. Back to where I don't have to risk my family's safety and well-being."

"You're afraid?"

David lifted Sarah's hands to his chest. The shame of what he was about to admit forced him to avert his eyes from hers. "I'm afraid I'll have to go to prison."

Sarah stepped closer, opening the hands she held against his chest. "Everything's happening so fast that I haven't thought about the risk. Do you think they'll bring Violet here?"

"I'm almost positive."

"But there were so many guards at the court house."

"I know, but Miss Johnson looked confident. And I

wonder how many of those guards are sympathetic to Violet. After all, Boston's the center of abolitionist activity."

*I brought him into this,* Sarah thought, bringing her cheek forward to touch his. *It's he who's taking the greatest risk. The courts were likely to be tougher on a husband than on the mother of a young baby. Yet how could they refuse a chance to save Violet?*

Sarah felt David's heart beating through his broadcloth shirt. *I love him so much. He's doing this because of me, because he knows I want him to.*

It wasn't fair. She had to hear that it was his own choice. "Do you want to back out?" she asked softly. "Because if you do, we can go to Miss Johnson's house right now and tell her we can't help. They'd still have all day tomorrow to come up with another plan."

David thought hard before he answered in a low whisper. "I don't want to back out. We have to help her."

"And the risk?"

"The early Christians had to risk everything just to worship." He sighed heavily. "I've had it easy all my life. Maybe it's time to find out how strong my faith is."

In the next room, Elsa was coaxing Eileen, who didn't want her eyes covered, to slip a cotton nightgown over her head. They were both sitting on Elsa's bed, and Eileen stubbornly shook her head every time Elsa brought the gown near her.

"Want to play 'peep eyes,' Eileen?" she asked. When the baby gave an expectant nod, she covered her own face with the gown. "Boo!" she exclaimed softly, letting the gown fall into her lap.

Eileen erupted into a fit of chuckles and pointed to

Elsa's face.

"You want me to do that again, don't you?" said Elsa.

After several episodes of this game, the baby pointed to the gown and her own face. "Leen," she said in an attempt to pronounce her own name.

"You want to hide from me?" As quick as a wink, Elsa had the gown over Eileen's head. "Boo!"

Eileen laughed until she started to hiccup, unaware that she'd been outsmarted. Elsa glanced at the door, wondering if the Adams's expected her to bring the baby out once she was finished.

*Maybe I should wait and let them come get her*, she thought. *Tension has filled the room ever since Mr. David and Miss Sarah returned from their outing. Maybe he's mad at her for asking me to come.*

She hoped not. Since they'd boarded the brig out of Charleston the previous morning, Elsa had almost felt like a young lady traveling with her family. David had pointed out several dolphins swimming alongside the ship and begging for scraps, and Sarah had told Elsa about her first travel by ship when she was sixteen. Eileen seemed to welcome her company, as well. She hadn't cried when her parents went out.

*They're not mad at me*, Elsa told herself sternly, trying to believe her own words. *Miss Sarah wouldn't have asked me to get the baby ready for bed if I wasn't doin' a good job. It's got to be something else.*

Whatever it was that was causing those two such concern, Elsa resolved to be an even greater help. *I'll keep my eyes and ears open, and if I see somethin' bad about to happen, I'll stop it somehow.*

The next morning, Sarah and David were awakened by church bells pealing out the Gloria Patri.

"We'd better get going," yawned David, rubbing the sleep from his eyes. Sunlight filtered in through the windows facing Massachusetts Bay, casting rectangular patterns against the opposite wall.

Sarah groaned. Eileen, unused to the new surroundings, had slept fitfully, crying out for her mother several times. Even Elsa in the next room had noticed, for she'd tapped on their door at about midnight, asking if she could help.

Raising her head to look at the sleeping form in the crib beside her, Sarah thought how easy it was to forgive a baby who looked like an angel. Brown eyelashes rested against smooth pink cheeks, and her lips were parted slightly from the pressure of the mattress.

At breakfast, David suggested they take a chaise to the Seamen's Bethel in North Square. "I've never been to Boston on Sunday," he said, "and I've always wanted to hear Edward Taylor preach."

"Who is he?" asked Sarah.

"He's a former sailor and pretty famous around here. They say seamen from all over attend his services. He has a place for them to stay while they're in port called the Mariners' House."

"Would you like me to keep Eileen here?" Elsa offered as she unfolded her linen napkin and placed it in her lap.

"Why, I wouldn't think of it," said Sarah. "The baby will be fine." Catching the crestfallen look that washed across the young maid's face, Sarah tried to identify its cause.

"Elsa," she began, removing her tea cup from Eileen's grasping reach, "is there some other congregation you'd rather visit? We could get you a carriage—"

"No, ma'am!" The girl's cheeks grew flushed. "I just ain't been to church since I moved away from Aunt Hattie's." At that, she'd only been to a couple funerals for some older relatives. She couldn't remember what the services had been like.

Sarah felt a stab of guilt. She'd been so busy during the short while that Elsa had been working for them that she'd not asked if the girl had a church. Willie Mae was a member of St. Michael's, and when Elsa disappeared on her full Sundays off, Sarah had assumed that she was going to church with the cook. It was on the tip of her tongue to ask Elsa where she spent her Sundays, but a second thought told her it would embarrass the girl.

"We'd love for you to go with us," she said, leaning forward. "Wouldn't we, David?"

David looked up from his eggs and bacon. "Of course." He gave Elsa a friendly wink. "You don't want to waste that pretty dress, do you?"

Elsa blushed. With her right hand, she touched the fine cloth of the blue calico dress Sarah had ordered for her before they'd left. "Thank you, sir," she mumbled, focusing her eyes on the gold rim of her bread and butter plate. She knew she could never be as beautiful as Miss Sarah, but it made her feel feminine to be complimented by a man, even though she knew he was just being nice.

"And thank you, Miss Sarah," she added timidly. "It's the most beautiful dress I ever owned."

"You're welcome." Sarah smiled at her. "It brings out the blue of your eyes."

Patting his mouth with his napkin, David said, "Are you three ladies about ready to get on our way?"

Elsa stood up, relieved. Whatever troubles had been

bothering Mr. David and Miss Sarah were apparently gone.

Edward Thompson Taylor walked the pulpit like a quarter-deck with a youthfulness that belied his fifty-plus years. Using a wealth of illustrations from the sea, he told his congregation that they came from "below—from under the hatches of sin, battened down above you by the evil one." Those who accepted Jesus as their Savior would one day go "aloft—with a fair wind—all taut and trim, steering direct for heaven in its glory, where there are no storms or foul weather, and where the wicked cease from troubling and the weary are at rest!"

Elsa sat wide-eyed through the entire service. Surely a person would have to be especially good before being allowed to ask Jesus to come into her life. According to the preacher who paced the platform before her, Jesus was God's own Son. Why would He be interested in the likes of her?

After church, they took a carriage to the Long Wharf, only a block from the hotel. Watercraft of all sizes dotted the blue-green horizon of the bay. Fishing boats were dwarfed by the towering masts, acres of canvas, and decorated bows of graceful clippers and rugged steamers.

"There she is, the *Knightsteed*," David said, pointing to a top-heavy clipper sporting the forepart of a horse for a figurehead. "She'll make the trip in about seventeen days, if the weather is good."

"Why, that's not long at all!" exclaimed Sarah.

"It's the sails that do the trick. The captain told me her mainmast is eighty feet tall, and she carries six thousand square yards of canvas. Our office is looking into using the clippers exclusively."

David carried Eileen in his arms, trying in vain to get her to look where he was pointing. A pair of sea gulls flapping overhead and screeching for handouts held her rapt attention.

"That'll be our home sweet home for a little while," he told Sarah. "Tomorrow, there'll be stevedores swarming all over her with their cargo loads."

"It's hard to believe we'll be on our way to England in less than two days," she said, shielding her eyes from the sun.

Giving a quick glance toward Elsa, who was several feet away emptying a pebble from her slipper, David lowered his voice. "Pray that nothing happens to change that."

Solemnly, Sarah nodded. Almost her every thought that day had been a prayer. "The Lord is going to watch over us and Violet," she said. "I can't explain it, but I feel a calmness that I didn't have last night. I think the Holy Spirit is telling us that we don't have to worry."

David gave her an affectionate smile. "I understand that feeling. When I first saw you those months after your husband had died, I'd been praying fervently that God would let me see you again. Then you walked into church, and suddenly I had an assurance that you'd one day be my wife."

With his fingertips, he caught a wisp of hair that the wind had blown across her face. "I've been too worried to have faith that God can get us through this. Thank you for reminding me."

Squinting at the early-afternoon sun, he said, "We'd better get back and give Eileen her nap."

## four

That evening, David ordered a light dinner of soup, bread, and cheese sent up to their suite, but no one had much of an appetite save Eileen. She perched, birdlike, on her mother's knee, popping open her mouth while Sarah fed her morsels of brown bread dipped in soup.

Elsa, who had a particular fondness for cheese, was too preoccupied to appreciate the rich flavor of the Camembert she'd spread on a slice of bread. Automatically she chewed, darting anxious glances at her employers.

She knew it was not her place to ask what was the matter. The curtain of gloom that had descended last night had returned, but this time it was different. She sensed anticipation in the air as well. Anticipation mixed with. . .hope?

Her questions were answered less than an hour later, after two white-aproned young men had cleared the table and taken the dishes from the room. Pushing back his chair a bit, David gave a meaningful look to his wife and then turned to the servant girl.

"Elsa," he began, his green eyes kind but serious. "I don't know if you've noticed, but Sarah and I have been under a strain since yesterday."

*What am I supposed to say?* the girl wondered. Never had an employer made so candid a statement to her. Mr. Clark had said barely four sentences to her the whole six years she'd been in his family's employ. Was Mr. David expecting her to pretend she hadn't noticed the tension, or did he want honesty?

They were watching her expectantly. Even baby Eileen, leaning back in her mother's lap, seemed to be waiting for an answer. *Say something now or they'll think you even more dull-witted than you are,* she ordered herself.

"Yes sir," she squeaked in reply. She stared at her hands, wishing she could disappear into the rosebud pattern of the carpet under her feet.

"I thought so," David said. "My wife and I have decided we must let you know why."

*Now I know I've done something!* Entwining her fingers in her lap so tightly that her knuckles were white, Elsa waited.

"We're concerned," David went on, "because you're probably going to be involved in something dangerous simply by being with us."

The word *dangerous* couldn't interfere with the elation Elsa felt once she knew she'd done nothing to displease the Adams. *When am I goin' to stop thinking that?* Relief and curiosity gave her enough courage to ask, "Involved, sir?"

"Yes." With a helpless smile, he said, "I wish I could tell you everything, but that's not possible. We're not sure ourselves what's going to happen. We suspect that a good friend of Sarah's is going to come here tonight."

"You're havin' a visitor sir?" *So that's why they seem to be waitin' for something to happen. But why the fear?*

David nodded. "A young Negro woman named Violet. She was a slave once, and she's in jail right now—at least we assume she is."

Sarah, who had gotten up to lay the now-sleeping baby in her crib, spoke as she sat back down in her chair. "Violet helped some runaway slaves escape, so she was arrested.

We think some friends of hers are going to break her out of jail tonight and bring her here."

Elsa's hand shot to her throat. "You're going to hide her from the law?"

A picture of her Aunt Hattie came to mind, laughing toothlessly at something she'd heard. *So your pappy thought he could keep runnin' from the sheriff, but he didn't reckon on those no-good friends of his turnin' him in for a few dollars!* she'd cackled with delight. *I wonder if he's findin' prison to his liking?*

"Yes, Elsa. That's what we're going to do," said David. "And if she needs to leave the country, we'll take her to England with us." He caught the quick motion of his wife's head. They'd only discussed hiding Violet for the night—he'd not allowed himself to think beyond that time—but now it made perfect sense. Searching Sarah's face, he was rewarded with a look of warmth and trust.

He blinked, remembering Elsa, and turned back to her. "We don't want to force you to be involved in something that frightens you. If you like, we can send you back to Charleston tomorrow. I'll send along a letter to my attorney, instructing him to pay your salary, and you can stay at the house."

The girl's face fell. "You mean, not go to England?"

David had to smile. "You really want to go, don't you?"

"Yes, sir! More than anything else in the world!" A crimson flush spread over her face. "That is," she added in a subdued tone, "if you and Miss Sarah want me to go."

"We don't know how we'd manage without you!" David said warmly.

"You've already been such a blessing," added Sarah. Her face became somber again. "Tell her the rest, David."

David nodded, his mouth set in a grim line. "We want you to do something for us." Bringing out a sealed envelope from the pocket of his waistcoat, he set it on the table.

"We don't look for any problems tonight when Violet comes, but it's wise to be prepared. In that envelope is the address of my family in Jasper, along with more than enough money to pay your passage."

"Sir?"

"This is in case something goes wrong. We'll be hiding Violet here until the day after tomorrow. If we're discovered, I'm going to insist that it's all my doing and that Sarah isn't involved. Sarah and you, of course."

Closing his eyes for a second, he sighed wearily. "I'm not sure that Sarah wouldn't be arrested as well because she's my wife. If she is, we want you to take Eileen to my family. There's a letter in the envelope asking them to let you stay with them as well. My parents are getting on in years. They'll need help with the baby."

Elsa's eyes were burning. She couldn't imagine either of them, especially Miss Sarah, going off to a damp, cold cell. People who did bad things belonged in prison, not anyone as kind and good as the Adams!

Suddenly she realized the huge responsibility they were willing to entrust her with—their own beloved child! *They wouldn't do that if they thought I was stupid. Were Aunt Hattie and Mrs. Clark wrong about me?* The thought was too much for her to absorb. Taking the envelope from the table, she held it tightly in her hand. "If you have to go to prison, I'll take good care of little Eileen."

She thought she heard a slight gasp from Sarah. "But I hope it don't come to that," she hastened to add. "And I'll help you hide your friend so nobody can arrest you."

The hours crawled by. Every time footsteps or voices sounded in the hall outside their suite, Sarah, David, and Elsa would freeze, ears straining. By the time ten o'clock came along, Sarah's hands were visibly trembling.

"I'm going to lie down," she told her husband. "If Violet comes and I'm asleep, wake me." Still in the dove-gray silk dress she'd worn to church, she slipped to the far end of the room.

Peering over the wooden crib, Sarah listened in the semi-darkness to Eileen's light snoring. She eased her arms under the baby's sleeping form and lifted her. Eileen whimpered a little while being carried to the bed, but settled back to sleep against her mother as they lay on top of the covers.

*Lord, please forgive me for having doubts again,* Sarah prayed. She moved her head forward to smell the child's soap-scented curls. *And please let me feel again the assurance that I felt this afternoon, that nothing is going to go wrong.*

David was at the window, and Elsa sat in an upholstered chair at the empty fireplace with a bit of embroidering in her lap.

"Elsa, you should get some rest," David said after checking his pocket watch again. "It's almost midnight."

The girl lifted her head. "Please let me stay up, sir. I want to make sure everything's goin' to be all right."

"If you wish," he said with a smile. "We can all catch up on our rest during the crossing—there's not a whole lot else to do."

"Can you tell me anything about England, Mr. David?" she asked shyly. "I don't know what to expect."

He tilted his head and thought. "It's quite foggy in some places, but it's got countryside that could take your breath away. There are beautiful old buildings—even castles. You'll be staying with Miss Sarah at the home of an old friend on the outskirts of Bristol. Her name is Julia Martin. I haven't met—" He stopped abruptly. The sound of a light footstep outside the door was clear.

Elsa had heard it too. As she stood, the embroidered handkerchief slipped from her lap.

The knock, when it came, caused them to jump. Giving Elsa a solemn glance, David crossed the room in an instant. "Yes?" he called softly.

"Your coat, mistah," came a young voice from the other side of the door. "My mammy done fixed that hole in the sleeve. She say you won't even know it was there, but you'd best be more careful with your cigars."

"What?" Unfastening the latch, David eased the door open and peered out. A slim black boy of indeterminable age stood in the hall, holding a wool frock coat across his arm. "I didn't have a coat repaired," David snapped. He was at once ashamed of the harshness of his voice. "You have the wrong room," he said in a kinder tone.

The boy grinned. "No, suh. I got the right room all right. And your wife done tole me you'd give me an extra dollah if I got it back to you 'fore midnight."

*Could this be part of the plan?* David wondered. It had to be, but what was his role? "Do you know my wife's name?" he whispered.

"'Course I do!" the boy said, making no effort to lower his voice. "Miz Adams be her name, and she say you gonna need this in a hurry 'cause you gone on a boat Tuesday mornin'."

Opening the door, David motioned the boy inside and peered down the lantern-lit hallway. It was empty. Closing the door, he turned to the boy. "Where's Violet?"

"Right here," came a womanly voice. The "boy" smiled. "Did I fool you, Mr. Adams?" she asked softly.

David let out a low whistle. "Violet?"

"I'm afraid so," she whispered back, a mischievous glint in her eyes. She glanced down at the worn suit she was wearing and patted the short woolly cap of hair on her head. "They had me dressed and shorn in such a hurry that I haven't looked in a mirror yet. It's worth it, though, to be out of jail. Where's Sarah?"

Motioning toward the far end of the room, David said, "She didn't get much sleep last night, so she laid down to rest. I'll go wake her up." When Violet protested, he added, "She asked me to. By the way, this is Elsa."

Elsa was still standing in front of her chair, her eyes wide.

"I'm pleased to meet you, Miss Elsa," Violet told her, taking a step in her direction.

"Just Elsa," managed the girl.

"All right. Please call me Violet." She lifted her arm and examined the frayed edge of her brown muslin shirt. "I sure do look more like a Fred or George right now."

Elsa had to smile at the woman's wit. She'd never been around black people much in her life. Yet Miss Sarah had said that Violet was her best friend, next to her husband. She felt a quick pang of envy for such a relationship. Elsa couldn't remember having a friend that close.

Sarah was up and ran to Violet with her arms open. "You're here!" she exclaimed wondrously. After a quick embrace, she took her by the shoulders and held her at arm's length. "At least I *think* it's you!

They pushed the four mahogany armchairs in a close circle so they could speak freely. Seated between Sarah and Elsa and across from David, Violet told them what she knew about her own escape.

"Lamps go out at eight o'clock in the jail rooms," she said.With her womanly voice and boy's appearance, Violet cut a comical figure. "I'd been told by Miss Johnson that something was gonna happen tonight, so I was a bundle of nerves. In spite of that, I fell asleep and they had to shake me awake."

"They?" asked David.

Violet grinned. "That big, mean guard with the bushy eyebrows. I thought he *hated* me, the way he used to glare every time he saw me! A colored woman I never met was with him—she cut my hair and helped me put on these clothes while he watched the door. It mighta taken her and me ten minutes from start to finish. Then the guard led me down the back staircase. A wagon was waiting."

Sarah shuddered. "Were you frightened, Violet?"

"I could hear my teeth rattling!" She stretched out a hand in front of her. "I'm still shaking a bit!"

Putting her hand back in her lap, Violet continued her story. "I crouched down amongst some boxes in the back of the wagon, with some feed sacks thrown over me. I didn't know who was driving 'til he let me out a half-block from the hotel. Turned out he was a member of my church."

"Why didn't he take you all the way here?" asked David.

"He told me that I'm supposed to be delivering some last-minute mending to the hotel, and that a colored delivery boy would usually be on foot."

Elsa had offered to go to her room before Violet began her narrative, but David had told her she was welcome to stay if she wished. Now she wondered if it would be all right to ask a question.

Violet noticed the puzzlement on Elsa's face. Smiling, she asked, "Is there something you're wondering?"

"Yes, m...ma'am," she stammered. "Why did you have to cut your hair and dress like a boy if nobody saw you?"

Violet nodded. "I was told it was in case somebody saw me in the hotel lobby or in the halls. Soon as the sun comes up, there's bound to be people looking for me and asking questions all over town."

"*Was* there anybody in the lobby?" asked David.

"Sure was. The man at the desk, and a couple of women were doing some cleaning."

"Won't they be expecting you to leave?"

With a chuckle, Violet said, "That's why I was so loud in the hall. One of the rooms on this floor was rented yesterday by an abolitionist friend of Mr. Garrison's. This morning a *real* boy about my size was smuggled into the room in a big trunk. When you let me in and closed the door, that was his signal to go down through the lobby."

Sarah drew her brows together. "Are you sure he did it? What if—"

"I had the same worry. I was full of questions when the driver let me out. He told me to do what he'd told me to do, and not to worry about the rest." Frowning, Violet put a hand in her coat pocket. "Oh, I forgot. The lady that helped me dress said to be careful, there's some money in here."

She brought out a wad of bills, then stood to hand them to David. "Will you count them, Mr. Adams? My hands are still shaking."

"Please call me David," he said. "And your friends are quite generous. You've got two hundred dollars here!"

To everyone's surprise, Violet looked stricken. "I can't accept that much money!"

"I'm sure it's to help you get settled somewhere," David explained.

"But that's money people donated to help the runaways!"

Sarah, exchanging a knowing look with her husband, spoke gently. "Violet, that's what they're using it for."

Violet shook her head. "But I'm not a runaway. I'm a free person of color, not a slave!"

David's face was grave as he leaned forward. "Violet, you're not going to be able to live in this country as a free person any more. You can be arrested in any state or territory, and your sentence will be much harsher since you escaped from jail."

After a long silence, the black woman's shoulders slumped. "Of course you're right. I guess I'll need to make my way up to Canada. It shouldn't be too hard, dressed like this."

"How about going to England with us?"

"Are you serious?"

Smiling, Sarah said, "We've already figured out how to make it work. We have four passages for our trip day after tomorrow: two regular tickets, one child's, and one servant's. She gave an apologetic look to Elsa. "That's how the company bought them. Servants traveling with their employers are charged half price. But your cabin would have been next to ours.

"Anyway," she went on, turning back to Violet, "You

can use the servant's passage. You'd have to pretend to be a slave again—but only for the time we're on the ship. We'll give Elsa money to buy her own passage before the ship leaves."

Elsa eased out the breath she'd been holding since Sarah had mentioned Violet using her passage. "I'll be glad to ride in the steerage, ma'am, to save you some money." She'd read about steerage in *Perilous Crossing*, one of the mystery novels she loved to pour over in the Harper Society Library, the only library in Charleston that was open on Sundays. While the cheap accommodations in steerage sounded unpleasant, she was so grateful the Adams were still taking her to England that she would have endured any hardship.

"There is no steerage compartment on this particular ship," David answered. "Most of its cargo is freight. Even if there was, we wouldn't think of letting you travel in it. You'll have your own cabin."

"But how will I help Miss Sarah with little Eileen?"

"During the day you can help out when Sarah needs you. It wouldn't look strange to have a single lady traveler befriend another lady on board. I know it sounds unnecessary to keep up the act once we leave Boston, but I don't want the authorities waiting for my wife and me when we get back to Charleston in a few months. We have to assume that at least one person on board will have heard about Violet's escape."

"I want to reimburse you for the extra ticket," Violet said.

David shook his head. "I appreciate that, but we can afford it." He held up his hand to her protests. "You'll need all your money to establish yourself somewhere in England."

"In England." Her face was doubtful now. "I realize that's what I have to do, so please don't think I'm not grateful to you both. It's just—"

"Just what, Violet?" asked Sarah. "Are you afraid?"

"No," she said hastily. Shifting in her chair, she added, "Well, yes. I'm afraid that there won't be any other Negroes in England."

Violet looked up at Sarah. "I feel like you're my sister, Sarah, and David, you're risking so much to help me. You're good people, and I'm blessed to be with you. But one day you'll go back home. I wish I could know that there are some other people there who look like me."

Brows knit together in concentration, David said, "I know I've seen some Negroes on my business trips over there."

"Many?"

"Not many, Violet. But what choice do you have?" Violet's abolitionist supporters must have planned on this. Hadn't Miss Johnson asked when they'd be leaving for England? And why hadn't they arranged for her to be smuggled to Canada or some other free country?

"I never saw a Negro until I came to America," Sarah was saying. "But I spent my whole life in two households in Bristol. I only went to the city once. We can ask people when we get there. My friend Julia Martin might know."

Violet gave a self-deprecating smile. "You must think I'm silly. Here I am, just out of jail and hiding from the law, and I'm worried about whether my sanctuary will be to my liking!"

Elsa had been absorbing only bits of the conversation for the last few minutes. She'd noticed an obvious gap in the plan to get Violet out of Boston. But if she asked more questions, would the Adams think she didn't know her place?

*You've got to stop being so timid!* she lectured herself. *If everything goes wrong, then she'll have to go back to jail and maybe Mr. David and Miss Sarah too.*

"Excuse me," Elsa said, clearing her throat. "What happens," she began, focusing her eyes on the painting above David's shoulder, "when Miss. . .when Violet is ready to leave? How is she going to get out of the hotel?"

David nodded at Elsa. "That's a good point." Turning to Violet, he asked, "Has that been figured out?"

"The driver told me that an hour before I'm ready to leave, one of you should open an east window and stand there for a little while with a white handkerchief in your hand. That'll signal them to send the boy back to the hotel and through the lobby."

"How will we know they saw our signal?"

"On his way down the hall, the boy's gonna give our door a single knock. Then he'll go into the same hotel room he came out of tonight. I'll have to leave pretty soon after that, and they'll carry the boy back out in a trunk sometime later." Her voice caught and her eyes grew moist. "I wish I knew his name. I don't know the names of most of the people who helped me."

"Perhaps they prefer it that way," Sarah said gently. "That way, if you were to. . .get caught, they wouldn't be discovered."

Violet wiped her eyes with the sleeve of her ragged coat. "Of course. That makes sense. I hope they know how grateful I am, and I hope you realize it, too. I know what a risk you're taking."

"We know that you'd do it for us if the situation were reversed." David covered a yawn with his hand. "I think it's time we were getting some sleep."

Standing, Violet agreed. "I've kept you good people up long enough. If you don't mind, I'll bed down on that sofa over there. Is there an extra pillow?"

"You can share my bed," Elsa said. "There's room for two, and a spare pillow."

Violet smiled at her. "Are you sure? 'Cause I really don't mind the sofa."

"I'm sure."

"I'll get you a nightgown," offered Sarah, coming to her feet as well. Her tired eyes held a mischievous glint as she studied Violet's clothes. "Or would you prefer one of David's nightshirts?"

"Sarah!" exclaimed David, his eyes widening. His face was flushed with embarrassment.

As if they'd practiced it, all three women covered their mouths with their hands, choking back the laughter that was begging to be released. After a few seconds of staring at them in shocked silence, the corners of David's mouth began to twitch. That triggered a fit of giggles in Violet, followed by Sarah and Elsa. Shaking his head, David grinned broadly.

When Sarah was finally able to speak, she said, "I'm sorry, David. I thought that Violet might want to stay in disguise all the time."

Violet held a hand to her aching side. "I'll take the nightgown, please. At least I can be a girl when I sleep!"

# five

"Tell me about yourself, Elsa," said Violet, clad in the green cotton shirt and tweed trousers that Sarah had bought for her before they left Boston. Violet and the young maid were seated with their backs propped against the wall on Violet's tiny berth. The *Knightsteed* had left Boston five days earlier, and while Elsa and Violet didn't dare socialize on deck, they spent a good deal of time together when they weren't helping tend to Eileen.

Unwrapping a handkerchief, Elsa took out a soft roll she'd saved from dinner, tore off a piece, and handed it to Violet. They'd both gotten wretchedly sick, as had David and Sarah and the baby, a couple days out of port when a terrifying storm struck. Sarah had advised them that keeping a little food in their stomachs all the time would help with seasickness, and it seemed to be working.

"There's not much to tell," Elsa answered. "My mother died when I was born, and I went to live with her aunt. When I was ten, I started working for the Clarks."

"What about your father?"

Elsa glanced at her hands. "Dead. At least that's what I hear." She hoped Violet wouldn't ask more about him because she'd have to tell Violet the truth. She'd pledged in her heart the day they'd gone to church in Boston that she'd be constantly good, so one day she wouldn't be ashamed to ask Jesus to be her Savior. Telling the truth was surely an important part of being good.

To her relief, Violet didn't press for details. "I don't remember my parents," she was saying with no trace of self-pity in her voice.

"You don't?" Elsa's eyes grew wide. "Who raised you?" As the words left her mouth she remembered that Violet had grown up a slave on a plantation.

"Different people. There was a cholera epidemic on the plantation where I was born. My parents died when I was three or four, and soon after that the owner went bankrupt and sold off his slaves. I worked for a family named Lucas until Mr. Bowman bought me."

"Miss Sarah's first husband?"

Violet gave her a sidelong look. "You know about him?"

"I know that he was the one who set you free."

Nodding, Violet said, "He did it because Sarah promised to marry him if he would. It hurt me to think about her marrying him 'cause of me, but God worked it out for the good. Right before he died, Mr. Bowman set all his slaves free in his will."

Elsa couldn't imagine anyone doing that. She'd seen placards advertising slaves all around Charleston—human labor was costly. "He must have been a real good man."

Giving her another look, Violet said, "He became a good man. I don't think Sarah would mind if I told you that he wasn't good until on his deathbed when he became a Christian. It shows you what our Lord can do."

"Well, if he was bad," said Elsa, confused, "how did he get to be a Christian?"

Violet hadn't meant to gossip about Jonathan Bowman, but Elsa's question made her glad the subject had come up.

Sarah had told her privately that she didn't know if Elsa understood about God's free gift of salvation. "You'll be able to spend more time alone with her than I will," Sarah had said. "Please talk to her about it, the way you explained it to me so long ago."

"You don't become a Christian by being good, Elsa." Violet's voice was filled with warmth. "None of us are good enough to earn salvation."

"Then how can we be saved?"

"By asking the Lord to let Jesus' dyin' on the cross be a sacrifice for our sins. Do you understand?"

Elsa's eyes looked glazed, but she answered, "Uh-huh."

"Do you really?"

Ashamed at herself for breaking her resolve to tell the truth, the girl shook her head.

Violet grinned. "Then why didn't you say so?"

"I didn't want to hurt your feelings."

"You ain't ever gonna hurt my feelings by being honest, child, but I'm touched that you care about them," said Violet. Wanting to explain salvation to Elsa, she asked, "You ever hear any Bible stories?"

"I don't think so," said Elsa. "Wait, is that story about a fish swallowin' a man in the Bible?"

"Jonah."

Elsa looked pleased. "Yes, that was his name. I read the story in a children's book at the library once."

"You can read?"

"Mildred, the cook at the Clarks' house, taught me so I could read the newspaper to her. The little letters in the paper gave her a headache."

"That's a shame, but it turned out to be a blessing for you, didn't it? Well, getting back to the Bible stories—a long time ago, people had to make sacrifices to God to cover up their sins. They'd take a lamb or dove or some other animal and offer it on an altar."

"You mean they'd kill it?"

"Real quick, so that it wouldn't be painful." The girl's face still looked shocked, so Violet added, "I don't understand all of it myself, but the Bible tells us that without the shedding of blood there's no forgiveness of sin."

"Then why don't people do that now? Sacrifices, I mean."

"Because God told people back then that one day He'd send a perfect sacrifice, His Son. That's why Jesus died on the cross and came back alive the third day—so we could have our sins forgiven."

Elsa looked thoughtful. "How do you become a Christian?"

"By asking Jesus to forgive our sins and to apply His sacrifice to them."

"That's all?"

Violet smiled. "That's all."

"Then why do people tell you to be good or you won't go to heaven?"

Violet shrugged. "I guess some people can't believe that they don't have the power to save themselves. If we could be saved simply by being good, then Jesus wouldn't have had to die on the cross."

"He wouldn't have?" asked Elsa.

"Do you think God would've let His Son suffer through all that misery if we could be saved another way?"

Hopefulness covered Elsa's face. "You mean I don't have to wait until I'm a better person? I can ask Jesus to be my Savior?"

"Of course you can!"

"Today?"

Touched by her sincerity, Violet asked, "How about right now?"

Elsa nodded, her heart thumping wildly in her chest. "Right now is fine. Please show me what to do."

Clasping her hands together in her lap, Violet bowed her head, and Elsa did the same. "Say what's on your heart, Elsa," whispered Violet.

Elsa opened an eye. "But what if I say the wrong thing?"

"There ain't no magic words. God's been drawing you to Him, or you wouldn't be interested in bein' saved. Now what do you want to ask Him?"

Elsa was silent for a full minute, then closed her eyes again. "I want to ask You, Lord Jesus, to forgive my sins and save my soul."

Again she was silent. Violet opened her eyes to see if something was wrong. Tears were streaking down Elsa's cheeks.

"Are you all right?" whispered Violet after a while.

Elsa blinked, as if startled that Violet was beside her. "I was thanking Him," she said, her face radiant.

Violet caught the girl in a hug. When she'd released her grip, she said, "Let's go tell Sarah and David!"


Unable to stand up to the dares and taunts of his mates any longer, the young sailor approached the woman standing at the corner of East Dock Road and Commerce Street. The sun had slipped into Bristol Channel hours ago, and the only obvious feature about the woman under the street lamp was a mass of flaming red hair.

With trembling hands, the boy rubbed his baby-smooth chin, trying to shut out all thoughts of what his mother back in Durham would think of what he was doing. His feet dragged woodenly over the cobblestones, and a queer sickness spread up from the pit of his stomach as he tapped the woman on the shoulder.

"Uh. . .Miss?" he said, his voice cracking.

With a rustle of skirts she turned to face him. "What can I do for you, dearie?" she asked with a leering smile.

That's when the boy noticed the smallpox scars that pitted her face. The amber glow of the street lamp turned her cratered skin sickly yellow.

"Sorry. I thought you were, uh, somebody else," he squeaked, backing up as he spoke.

The woman's eyes narrowed, and she heard hoots of laughter in the alley. "Get out of here, you scrawny little pup!" she screamed at the terrified adolescent.

Stumbling over his feet, he turned and ran.

The woman spat upon the cobblestones in the direction of his fading footsteps. Young snits. They were all alike! After they spent years working on ships, when their skin turned to leather and their teeth rotted, they weren't so choosy. She didn't need any of those pasty-faced tots to provide her with a living!

Still, it was getting late, and she cast anxious eyes down the darkened East Dock Road. Raymond would probably beat her if she came home without enough money for liquor. Sometimes he beat her when she did.

Across the street, the doors swung open to The Tidy Buckett, belching music and raucous laughter into the night air. A seaman of indeterminate age was leaving the gin palace. He took swaying steps toward the street, stopping to grab a post for support. Steadying himself, he was about to take another step when he doubled over and threw up on the porch boards.

The corners of the woman's mouth curled as she gathered up her skirts to walk across the street. Raymond would have his gin.


On the evening of September seventh, eighteen days after she had left Boston, the *Knightsteed* made it to the quay of Bristol. Because she carried mainly cargo such as cotton and rice, the ship was moored at a commercial landing in front of a huge warehouse.

Sarah carried the chattering, wide-eyed Eileen across the boarding ramp with Elsa at her side. Violet, clad in boy's clothes, followed at a respectful distance. David was below, arranging to have their trunks and valises brought on shore.

"I feel like I'm going to topple over any minute," said Elsa when they'd stepped onto the weathered boards of the dock.

Sarah laughed. "Me, too."

The girl watched her with concern. "Please take care that you don't drop the baby."

Holding her daughter more tightly, Sarah shot Elsa a grateful look. "We'll get our land legs back in a little while. What do you think of England?"

"England?" Elsa had been so worried about Eileen that she hadn't looked past Sarah's shoulder. Gazing at the sights, she was overwhelmed with awe. A row of Georgian houses perched high above the harbor. Warehouses as massive and exotic as Egyptian temples rose out of the streets, and steep, green hills encompassed the city. "It looks—pretty."

"It is in the few places that I've seen," Sarah told her. "And wait until you see the countryside." They had reached Wharf Street, and Sarah motioned to the driver of a waiting town coach.

"My husband will be here soon," she said to the portly man, impressive as an army general with his uniform of top boots, white leather breeches, striped waistcoat, dark blue coat, and top hat. Scrambling down from his perch with surprising agility, he helped them into opposite seats in the enclosed carriage.

When Violet approached, the man hesitated. Turning his face toward Sarah, he waited for instructions.

"Lazarus will ride in here with us," she said.

When Violet had settled in the seat next to Elsa, she leaned forward to glance out the door. The driver was with the two horses, adjusting one of the harnesses. "Lazarus?" she whispered to Sarah.

Sarah looked sheepish. "I was reading the book of John in my Bible last night. It was the only name I could think of in a hurry."

"I guess it could have been worse," Violet said with a wry grin. "You could've been reading Daniel, and called me Nebuchadnezzar or Belshazzar!"

"Maybe we should think of a boy's name for you," Elsa suggested, "so we won't end up callin' you different names at the same time. That might look odd to people."

"No thank you!" Violet's mouth was set. "David said I wouldn't have to wear these awful breeches once we got away from the ship."

David came along then, dressed in a gray tweed coat and cord trousers. "The steward will have our things delivered to our hotel within the hour," he said, waving away the driver's offer to help as he swung himself into the carriage.

David and Sarah had decided on the ship that, since he had immediate business in Bristol, they would stay in a hotel in town the first few days. After that, Sarah, Eileen, Violet, and Elsa would stay with Julia Martin while David went on to Liverpool for a fortnight.

With a creak of metal against wood, the chaise began to move. Violet studied David anxiously. "Will I be allowed to stay at the hotel?"

"I'm not sure, Violet. I was wondering that myself." He ran a hand through his sandy-colored hair. "Port cities are used to people of different races, so it might not cause a problem. If it does, we'll find another place or stay at Miss Martin's."

Giving him a grateful look, Violet turned her attention to the quaint streets and buildings of Bristol. *Is this where I'm destined to spend the rest of my life? Will I be able to find a job?* David had told her that the town's cloth trade, though not as heavy as it had been fifty years earlier, was still important. She hoped that meant she'd be able to find a position as a seamstress. She loved the feel of fine silk, cashmere, challis, or crepe de chine under her nimble fingers as she fashioned it into stylish dresses.

Past the warehouses, the town was a mixture of new and old. Scores of century-old gabled houses with round narrow courtyards lined Palmer Road. Three blocks away from the wharf area, the coach stopped in front of a wide, two-story hotel of gray brick. Green shutters stood guard at every window. Over the glass and wood door hung a scrolled sign identifying the Palmer House Inn.

Reserving a suite was no problem, even though the proprietor could see that Violet was with them. By the time they'd checked in and had gone up to the rooms, Sarah was intent on going straight to bed. Eileen had fallen asleep in the carriage, and her head rested against her mother's shoulder.

"I'm tired too," agreed David. The suite had a separate sitting room with two bedrooms. He walked over to his and Sarah's room and opened the door for her. "It always takes me a few days to recover from a crossing." Turning to Violet and Elsa, he asked, "Would you ladies like me to order some supper for you?"

"No thank you," Elsa answered.

"None for me neither," Violet answered, covering a yawn. "I believe I'll turn in, too, so's I can go shopping for a dress tomorrow. Can't look for a job in these clothes." She held up a hand when she saw that David was about to speak. "I appreciate what you're about to offer, but you've spent enough on me. I'll buy my own dress, my friend."

"Would you like me to go with you, Violet?" asked Elsa. "That is, if Miss Sarah don't need me."

They heard a click as David closed the door. Taking a step toward the bedroom they were to share, Violet answered, "That would be fun. But aren't you going to go to bed, too?"

Elsa shook her head. "This is the first time I ever been anywhere away from Charleston, besides Boston. I'm too excited to sleep."

"What are you gonna do?"

Motioning toward a gold sateen-covered chair, she said, "I'll probably pull this up to a window and watch the city."

Violet nodded, her hand on the door. "Elsa," she asked, "are you happy?"

The girl paused from tugging on the armchair and looked up. "Happy?"

Folding her arms, Violet said, "I'm just wondering. If

I'm being too nosy—"

"You're not bein' nosy," she answered. "I just never asked myself that question. Come to think of it, I s'pose I am." She tilted her head and gave Violet a wondrous smile. "Ain't that something?"

Though she'd sat up half the night, Elsa was the first one awake the next morning. She could understand why the others were sleeping in. The berths aboard ship had been narrow and hard, not conducive to rest.

Too modest to wear her wrapper in the hallway, she put on a clean dress from her trunk, then slipped out of the living room and into the carpeted hallway. The water closet was next to the staircase at the end of the hall. Once inside, she undressed down to her slip, cleaned her teeth, and sponge-bathed. Dressing again, she made her way toward the staircase.

Not since she'd gathered the courage to slip out of the Clarks' house and apply for a position with the Adams had she ever done anything so daring. Having lived with rejection, she'd learned not to put herself at risk by seeking the company of others.

Spending so much time with Sarah and David and Violet had given her the beginnings of self-confidence. *If they don't think I'm stupid and ugly, perhaps I'm worth something after all,* she reasoned. *Besides, Jesus didn't turn me down when I asked Him to be my Savior.*

Elsa practically floated down the stairs, not bothering to hold the railing. The staircase ended in the hotel's main lobby, resplendent with Brussels carpets and a sparkling crystal chandelier of at least a hundred candles. Elsa had been too worried about whether Violet would be allowed to stay with them to pay much attention to her surroundings when they'd checked in. She stood directly under the chandelier and looked up at it. *I'll come back down here tonight and see it when it's all lit up,* she told herself. *Maybe Miss Sarah will let me bring Eileen, too.*

Though it was early, a good number of people were in the lobby. Some were at the desk transacting business, and others were entering the dining room through a big doorway to the left of the staircase. Still others sat on the upholstered sofas and visited or read newspapers. Elsa's ears picked up at the strange language coming from a nearby family seated on two settees facing each other. *French*? she wondered.

After a few minutes of people-watching, Elsa decided to go outside. As she approached the front door, a doorman in a blue and gold tasseled uniform with white-stockinged calves, opened the door. His slight bow as she passed made her feel important, and she gave him a smile.

Stepping from under the striped canopy over the front door, Elsa felt a fine rain, just enough to cool her face and hands. The street noises were loud as the city came to life. Great dray horses pulled sledges and carriages along the cobblestones, and a number of people passed on foot.

A voice caught her attention, out of place among the street sounds. Her first impulse was to go inside, for there'd been a threatening note in that voice. Curiosity got the better of her, and she followed the sound to the corner of the hotel building. She peered around the side.

"Dumb-dumb Danny-boy!"

What Elsa saw chilled her. Ten feet away, a group of four boys, probably none older than twelve, surrounded the bottom of a wooden ladder. Laughing and taunting, they didn't notice her as they took turns shaking and kicking the ladder's rungs. At the top of the ladder, propped under a second floor window was a young man, clutching the window ledge with his fingers. His face was white as paste, and he stared down in agony at his tormentors. On the ground sat an overturned metal bucket. Patches of suds were sinking into the grass.

Too outraged to be afraid, Elsa marched over to the boys. She grabbed one by the shoulders and pulled him away with enough force to send him sprawling back on the ground.

"Hey, whut are you doin', lady!" exclaimed a gap-toothed boy with blond hair. His arms were still wrapped around the rail he'd been shaking.

"Stop that right now!" she hissed though clenched teeth while reaching out to pull his arm away. The other two boys, much younger, glanced at each other and took a step back.

The boy she'd pushed down was back on his feet, coming at her with a rock the size on an egg in his hand. "You'd better get outta here right now!" he yelled, cocking back his arm menacingly.

Quick as thought, Elsa had him by the tip of the nose. "Or you'll what?" she asked, squeezing her fingers together.

"Hey, let my bruther go!" The boy who'd had his hands on the ladder was at her side now, tugging at her elbow.

"Not until he hands me the rock." Narrowing her eyes, she tightened her grip on his nose.

"Ow!" wailed the boy. His eyes were rimmed with tears. "Lemmegopease!"

"Give me that rock!" Elsa commanded. "Or I'm going to lead you right to the police!" She hoped the boy wouldn't call her bluff, for she had no idea where the police were located in this strange town.

The boy held the rock out to her in his open palm. Elsa snatched it with her left hand and let go of his nose.

"Now, get away from here, and don't let me catch you pickin' on anybody again! You could've hurt him bad!"

The red-nosed boy was about to speak but thought better of it. His mouth snapped shut.

"Come on," his brother said, motioning to the two younger boys. "This ain't fun, anyhow." Without a word to Elsa, the boys sprinted off. When they were a safe distance away, the boy she'd pinched yelled an obscenity at her.

Resisting the urge to pitch the rock at the small of his back, Elsa turned her attention to the young man on the ladder. All she could see was a shock of unruly brown hair as he clung to the window ledge. She suspected he was different, like George, the man who swept the streets in Charleston. People called George an idiot, but he had always remembered her name, greeting her every time he saw her.

"They're gone now," she called up to the boy. "Are you all right?"

He sobbed softly.

"Let me hold the ladder steady and you can climb down," she called again.

"Can't," came the voice.

"Yes you can! I'll make sure that you don't fall."

There was a long pause. Speaking so softly that Elsa had to cup her hand behind an ear to catch his words, the boy said, "Are you gonna be mad at me?"

"Be mad at you? Of course not! Why would I be mad?"

A great sob tore from the boy. He rested his head against the top rung, not looking at her. "'Cause I wet my pants."

Elsa's heart went out to the boy. "I ain't goin' to be mad

at you," she called up to him gently. "You had an accident 'cause you were scared. That's nothing to be ashamed of. Now will you please come down?"

Whimpering, he eased a foot down to the next rung. Elsa wrapped both arms around the ladder and held on, mindful that any movement could cause him to panic and lose his grip. When he reached the last two rungs, she moved out of the way.

As soon as his feet touched the ground, the boy turned his back to her. "Thank you," he said over his shoulder, sniffling as he spoke.

Wishing that she'd brought a handkerchief, Elsa asked, "Is there anything I can do for you?"

"Mr. Harold will be so mad at me if I don't wash them windows," he moaned, turning his head enough so that he could watch her from the corner of his eye. Elsa guessed that he was about her age. The only thing that set his profile apart from normal was the way he held his mouth slack when he wasn't speaking. Of medium height, he had shoulders that drooped slightly.

"Why don't you finish?" Elsa asked. "I'll stay and hold the ladder for you as long as I can."

"I have to change my clothes."

"Do you have a room here?"

The boy nodded. "Up in the attic. It's a real nice room and it's all mine."

Elsa smiled. "I imagine it's nice. I had an attic room for a long time, but I had to share it with another maid."

"You did?" In his excitement, the boy wheeled around to face her. "Did you ever look out the window and see the moon?"

Before Elsa could answer, the boy remembered why he'd had his back to her. With a yelp of embarrassment, he dropped to his knees, trying to cover his body with his arms.

"Look, I'll turn around this time," Elsa said calmly, turning her back to him. "I don't think you wet your pants, though."

"I didn't?"

"I don't think so. I think you sloshed some water on yourself before your bucket fell."

Silence was broken by the boy's laugh. "That's what I did!" he exclaimed. "Now I remember!"

Turning back to face him, Elsa joined in the laughter. The boy was so pleased, he was hugging himself and rocking on his heels. "I didn't have a accident," he said over and over.

"Is your name Danny?" Elsa asked when the laughter had subsided.

He looked surprised. "Do you know me?"

"Those bad boys—I heard them call you that."

Danny's gray eyes grew wide, and he glanced around fearfully.

"Don't worry. They're gone," she reassured him.

"You made them go away," he said. "You're nice."

"Thank you." Elsa reached for the bucket on the ground and handed it to him. "Why don't you hurry and get some more water so I can keep the ladder steady for you."

"Okay." Swinging the pail at his side, Danny started loping down a brick walkway leading to the back of the hotel. When he reached the corner, he turned back. "What's your name?" he called.

"Elsa."

"Good name," he called back before disappearing around the corner.

## *six*

At the sound of the door opening, Sarah looked up from where she'd been playing with Eileen. "Did you sleep well?" she asked her husband as he came through the door from their room.

Smiling, David came over to them and got down on one knee. "I didn't mean to sleep so late. It seemed all night that I could still feel the motion of the ship." Bending, he kissed first her cheek, and then Eileen's. "How long have you been awake?"

"About an hour. We saved you some rolls and marmalade."

Eileen reached for her father's hand, pulled herself to her feet, and pointed to the nearest window. "See," she said, tugging at his hand.

"You want to show Daddy something?" Giving Sarah a wink, he let the little girl guide him to the window. Picking her up so they both could look out, he said gently, "Yes, I see the buildings."

Eileen leaned her curly head forward until her forehead touched the glass. "Go?"

"She's looking for the boy who was cleaning the windows when we first got up," Sarah explained. "He was making faces at her to make her laugh, and I think she wants him to come back and play."

"He's gone bye-bye," said David, bending down to set Eileen back on her feet.

"Bye-bye?"

"Yes, but I'll bet we've got a doll around here some-where." His eyes scanning the room, David caught sight of the hand-made rag doll Violet had sent them after Eileen was born. He went over to pick it up, then put it in her upstretched arms. "That's it, play with your doll," he said.

As the baby sat down on the carpet to play, David offered Sarah his hands. He caught her up in his arms as he pulled her to her feet. "How's it feel to be back home?" he asked as they stood with their arms around each other.

"Home?" she murmured into his ear. "My home is wherever you are."

His arms tightened around her. "Sometimes it scares me, how happy I am. I don't know what I'd do without you and Eileen."

"And you'll never find out. God kept us together and safe in Boston when we could have been caught any moment, and He's going to keep watching over us."

"You're right," David whispered. "You're a strong woman, Sarah, to have so much faith."

His words surprised her. "If I have any strength," she told him, "it's because I feel secure. You take good care of us."

Eileen, tired of playing with the doll, was at their knees trying to squeeze between them. "Up?" she said, holding out her arms.

With a chuckle, David reached down to lift her, then brought her over to sit on his knees on the sofa. "Are Violet and Elsa still asleep?"

"They left after breakfast to buy Violet some clothes," Sarah answered, taking a seat beside them. "About ten minutes before you got up."

"How is Violet going to shop for lady's clothes when she's dressed like a boy?"

"I'm not sure, but they'll figure something out. I offered to lend her one of my dresses, but she's so much slimmer and shorter than I am."

David bared his teeth and growled at Eileen, who had been trying to get her fingers in his mouth ever since they sat down. With an excited squeal, she dove head first into her mother's lap.

"Why don't we go for a stroll after lunch?" asked David. "There are parts of town I've never seen.

"Don't you have to go to work?"

"Tomorrow's soon enough to start all that. Right now I want to show off the two most beautiful ladies this side of the Atlantic."

Celly sauntered down Palmer Road, her nose in the air and scarlet ringlets of hair flying in every direction. Her lips pressed together tightly.

*He'd promised he wouldn't play Hazard with those rakes again!* she fumed. Every time Raymond picked up a set of dice it cost her. Now she was the one who had to worry about raising the money while Raymond slept off his drink.

*I should go somewhere else and let him face them tonight empty-handed! He'd learn a good lesson about listening to what I say!* Of course, he'd probably be dead if he couldn't produce at least half of what he owed them.

She squinted her eyes, not used to the afternoon sun. If it weren't so early in the day, she could raise the money herself. Night, though, was when she practiced her trade, stalking the darkened streets and alleys after men had their eyesight blurred in the gin palaces and rum houses.

Two staid younger ladies stood on the sidewalk in front of a millinery shop, frozen wide-eyed while they watched Celly's advance. Lowering her head, she hastened her steps and barreled toward them, causing them to jump back to keep from being trampled. As she passed she threw a vulgar epithet their way, then grinned as she imagined the shock it must have brought to their powdered, lily white faces.

Finally she reached the Palmer House Inn. She knew better than to try to enter—the stuffy old steward had threatened to send for the police if she ever came inside. Crossing the street in front of the hotel, she stood under the awning of a bakery.

*Surely Danny'll come out soon.* Celly hoped she wouldn't have to wait too long. She could use another five or six hours of sleep before work began. Danny delivered messages for the steward sometimes, so she kept her eyes glued on the wide front door across the street.

Thirty minutes later, she was still waiting, anxiously shifting her weight from one foot to the other every time someone walked out the door. She was toying with the idea of hiring some street kid to go inside and deliver a message, when the door opened again and a handsomely dressed couple came walking out, the man carrying a baby.

Disappointed, Celly let out a snort of disgust. Then she realized that the woman was looking her way. There was something familiar about her.

"David, I think that lady wants to speak with us," whispered Sarah. "See, she's staring straight at us."

With Eileen at his shoulder, David glanced across the

street, then offered his wife his free arm. "No, I'm sure she's waiting for someone else. Let's go this way."

Taking her husband's arm, Sarah couldn't resist one last look at the woman. She had known someone with hair that color a long time ago, a spiteful girl named Celly. She'd caused Sarah's mother to lose her job.

*That can't be her, though. Celly was pretty, and just a bit older than me. This poor woman looks at least thirty years older.*

"David, she's watching us again," Sarah said. "Perhaps she needs some help."

David pressed her arm closer to his side, hastening her along as they walked in the opposite direction. "She needs some help all right," he muttered.

Recognition narrowed Celly's eyes into slits. *It's that prissy-faced cook's brat! What was her name?* She chewed on her lip but couldn't come up with the name. *Don't matter. How dare she look at me with pity! Her with her fancy clothes and fancy husband and baby! What did she know about working hard for every scrap of food?*

Her hands clenched into fists. *Sarah Brown—that's her name! It was her fault that I couldn't get a decent job.* Standing on the sidewalk, Celly glared at David and Sarah's backs until they were out of sight.

Celly had been sixteen and a maid in the Norton household where Sarah's mother, Ruth, was employed as the cook. After watching her boyfriend stutter and preen around the girl Sarah, Celly had decided to get rid of her. One day while the Nortons were away on holiday, she'd crept into their youngest daughter's room, stolen her most treasured doll, and hid it under Sarah's bed.

Her plan had worked. Sarah and her mother had been

dismissed when the doll was discovered. A few days later, Celly had sneaked too much cooking sherry from the new cook's supply and had laughingly confessed to another servant that she'd stolen the doll. The traitor had told Mrs. Norton, who fired Celly and refused to give her a letter of reference.

Celly had laughed at them all when she realized she could make more money hanging around street corners than she'd ever made as a servant. Two years later she'd contracted smallpox and nearly died. The scars had ruined her good looks. Her income dropped drastically, and she was reduced to living in a crumbling tenement.

*That simpering lady dares to look down on me! If her husband wasn't with her I'd. . .I'd pull the hair out of her fine head—all of it! Then we'd see how she likes havin' people stare at her!*

Caught up in her bitterness, Celly suddenly realized that Danny had left the hotel and was heading down the street. His gait, though awkward and loose-jointed, was swift, and she had to run to catch up with him.

"Hallo-o-o, Danny!" she called.

He stopped and turned slowly, an uncertain look on his face. Realizing who was following him, Danny broke into a huge grin. "Hey, Miss Celly!" he called, waving eagerly.

Miss Celly was nice to him most of the time—much nicer than his brother, Raymond. Before Danny had gotten the job at the hotel and moved into his attic room, Celly would take him places and get him to sing for people. It had been great fun. Everybody had laughed and been so happy. The only bad part had been when they'd given him things to drink that he didn't like. He'd tried to tell them he didn't want any, but they'd act so hurt. Miss Celly would look like she was going to cry, so he'd finally drink whatever it was, holding his nose and trying not to gag.

Celly had caught up with Danny. Smiling, she patted his shoulder. "How are you doing, Danny?"

"Doin' good," he said. "I washed the windows."

"That's nice." She turned her head to look back at the hotel. "And don't they look clean!"

Blushing with pleasure, Danny waited for Celly to continue.

Her face had lost its smile when she turned back to him. "I'm worried about your brother. He's sick, and we ain't got the money to buy medicine."

Danny looked stricken. "Is he gonna die?"

"Not if we can get him some medicine. I don't know where we're going to get some money, and he feels awful poorly."

Danny shoved his hands in his pockets, drawing his eyebrows together as he tried to think. He had some coins in his room, but he'd been saving them for weeks to buy a big glass bowl with some goldfish inside. Miss Abby, the scullery maid, had counted his money for him and told him if he saved for one more week he'd have enough.

"Danny?"

Shame caused him to lower his eyes. His brother was dying, and all he cared about was his fish. "I got some money," he mumbled around the lump in his throat. "I was gonna buy some goldfish, but I don't want Raymond to die."

Celly leaned forward and planted a kiss on Danny's cheek. "I daresay he'll be better by tonight! Now run and get me the money, and I'll wait right here."

Folding her arms across her buxom chest, Celly sat

down on the wooden bench in front of the apothecary. For
the hundredth time, she wondered why she didn't leave
Raymond. Despite her homely looks, she could have
another man to take his place within a day or two. But why
bother? The men who hung around the rum houses and gin
palaces were all alike.

She remembered how nice-looking the man walking
with Sarah had been—not handsome, but well dressed and
clean. Prosperous, too. He didn't look the type to beat on
women. No, he probably treated her like a queen, and a
fragile one at that, giving her flowers and little gifts.

*I could have had a life like that, too,* Celly thought. *If
Sarah hadn't flirted with my boyfriend and made me mad
enough to hide that doll, I wouldn't have caught smallpox.
I was pretty when I worked for the Nortons. I might have
met a nice, rich man on my half-day off.*

Occupied with her envy and growing hatred, Celly
didn't hear Danny until he was standing in front of her.
Solemnly he held out a painted tobacco tin.

Celly grabbed the tin, lifted its lid, and peered inside.
"Are you sure you don't have more?"

"No, ma'am. Is that enough to buy medicine?"

"Barely." Celly snapped the lid shut. "Your brother will
appreciate it." She was about to take her leave when a
thought occurred to her. "Danny, there's a young man and
woman with a baby staying at the hotel. The man has light
hair, and the woman's hair is dark brown, like the baby's.
Do you know who they are?"

Danny thought hard, then his face brightened. "Some
people came last night that look like that. I seen a baby and
the mama when I washed the windows." Smiling wistfully, he added, "I made the baby laugh."

"I'll bet you did," Celly muttered. She gave him a warm smile. "What room are they in, Danny?"

"Room? The one upstairs."

Keeping the smile frozen on her face, she asked though her teeth, "Which room upstairs?"

Frustration came to his eyes. "The one at the corner, the soot."

"They're in a suite?"

Relieved, Danny nodded. "A soot."

Suppressing her frustration, Celly kept a patient expression on her face. "Is there a number on the door?"

"Uh-huh. There's a *two* and a *one*." Danny looked back to the hotel. "I've got to take Mr. Harold's letter to the post office," he said. "He'll be mad if I take too long."

Celly ignored his worries. "You mean, a *twenty-one*, right?"

"No, just a *two* and a *one*. Can I go now?"

"In a minute. How about stairs. Is there a back stairway for the servants?"

Danny nodded once more, looking over his shoulder at the hotel. "Back stairs."

"How do you get to them, Danny?"

"Next to the kitchen." Tears filled his eyes. "Can I go now, Miss Celly?"

Smiling, Celly stood and patted him on the shoulder. "Yes, you can go, Danny. You've been a good boy."

Thirty minutes later, she was walking down Benton Street, too narrow for anything but foot traffic. Passing gin-palaces, sailors' boarding houses, coffee shops, fish markets, and dancing saloons, Celly stopped in front of a dingy establishment with crude letters declaring Used Clothes.

*I'm gettin' tired of Raymond,* she thought, making a fist around the thirty-two shillings Danny had given her. *Wonder how long it took the dummy to save this up?*

A woman wearing dark rouge and a hideous black wig hurried to the front of the shop when Celly entered.

"I'm looking for a mourning dress, and I'll need a hat and veil to go with it," Celly announced. "Do you have anything that'll fit me?"

The woman came to life, pointing toward one of several heaps of clothes on the floor. "Dresses over there," she said, "Got one yesterday—won't last long."

Celly began to dig through the wrinkled dresses, most reeking of body odors and filth. She hated to touch anything in the place, but she had neither the time nor the money to have a decent dress made. *For all I know, they could check out of the hotel in the morning,* she·thought with a frown.

Finally she found the black muslin dress. All its buttons were intact. Fearing lice, Celly held the dress as close to her waist as she dared. It would be tight, for her waist had thickened over the years, but it would do.

"Now," she said, turning to the woman. "The hat and veil?"

The woman went to a shelf piled with hats and picked out a slightly misshapen black silk hat with a new veil. The coal-shuttle style announced that the hat was at least ten years old. "Got it yesterday."

*Yes, and the dress too,* Celly thought cynically. "How much?"

"Fifteen shillings for the lot."

Celly gave a snort of disgust. "I'll do you a favor and give you ten."

"Twelve."

"Never mind," said Celly, dropping the dress back on the pile of clothing.

"I'll take ten," the woman hastened to say.

"When can you have it washed and pressed?"

"Day after tomorrow, if it don't rain. Cost you four pence extra."

"Make it look nice and I'll give you six." Celly counted out ten shillings and put them in the woman's upturned palm.

"You goin' to a funeral?" the woman asked, slipping the coins in her apron pocket.

Celly had started for the door. "Going to visit an old friend," she threw over her shoulder.

## seven

"What about here?" asked Violet, pointing to a white-washed storefront on Redcliffe Street, set between a pottery shop and a bakery. There was no sign over the door, but a dress hung in the polished glass window.

"Here?" Elsa peered into the window, then wrinkled her nose. "It don't look like a very busy place. I don't know why you didn't like that other shop. The sign said their prices were cheap." What cheap meant in Bristol she had no way of guessing. The first time she'd realized that the British had a different currency was when Violet had gotten some money transferred at the hotel desk just before they left.

"Yes, but they're too busy. I can't wait two weeks to get a dress, and nobody's likely to hire me in these clothes."

"Miss Sarah said you could cut down one of hers."

"Sarah's done enough for me," said Violet. "I don't want to ruin one of her dresses."

"Then how about one of mine? I know you like that blue one."

Violet shook her head. "Thank you, child, but you don't have enough dresses to be giving any away. I'll be fine if I can find somebody who'll work fast."

"I guess it's hard to please a seamstress, ain't it?" Elsa asked affectionately.

Shrugging her shoulders, Violet said, "After I get a job I'll make my own clothes, like I did before. I sure wish I had some of them with me now."

Eyeing the lengthening shadows, Elsa nodded. "We'd better hurry. Are you ready, Mr. Lazarus?"

They had a system worked out. Elsa, carrying a slip of paper with Violet's measurements, said she was looking for a dress for a friend, which indeed she was. Violet allowed people to assume she was Elsa's servant, brought along to carry packages.

"I'm ready," she answered. "Remember, if I cough, I don't like the fabric."

Elsa smiled. "I remember. The woman in that other shop must'a thought you had consumption!"

Returning her smile, Violet said, "You know, you're fun to be with."

"Me?"

"Yes. Didn't you know that?"

Elsa shook her head, incredulous. "Nobody ever told me that. You mean, you're glad I came with you?"

"Of course I am. Now let's go find a dress."

The tiny shop was brightly lit but empty of customers. Sketches of ladies wearing stylish gowns were hung at eye-level on the wall, and samples of fabrics were arranged on a low table.

"Vhat may I do for you, miss?" A mournful man with a bushy, iron-gray beard pushed his chair away from a desk in the far corner of the shop. As he approached, he appeared startled to see Violet but recovered in time to give them a weary smile. "You vould like a dress?"

"I'm lookin' for a dress for my friend," Elsa explained.

"You are from America?"

"Yes sir—just last night." *No wonder I'm so tired!* she thought. She'd put in a full day of activity after only a few hours of sleep. Stifling a yawn, she explained, "My friend needs the dress as soon as possible, and while not too expensive, it must be attractive and well made." Violet had given her the words to say, and Elsa liked the way they sounded. They made her feel educated, refined.

The mournful face grew even more so, as the man tugged thoughtfully on his beard. "Can your friend come here for measuring tomorrow? That is vhen my assistant vill be present."

"I have the measurements here," Elsa replied, handing him the slip of paper. "It won't be possible for her to come in. When do you think you could have one ready?"

"In three days after the measuring, I belieff, if your friend is in a hurry. I do not see vhy it cannot be ready by then."

Elsa caught the nod of Violet's head and turned back to the man. "May we. . .I see some fabric samples and patterns?"

"Yes, of course. I haff some dresses that are vaiting to be picked up. Perhaps you vould like to look at them, to give you an idea?"

When Elsa agreed, the man offered them two chairs and disappeared through the curtain-covered doorway. Less than a minute later he was back with two dresses draped across his arms. One was a mauve sateen ball gown trimmed with lace, and the other an attractive lavender dress made of chambray. Setting the gown on a wooden stool, he took the dress by the shoulders and let it fall open to the carpet in lavender folds.

"This is very pretty." Elsa reached down and brought the hem of the dress to her lap. Turning it inside-out, she was careful to hold it where Violet could see the workmanship.

Uneven stitches in the seams filled her with disappointment. Any dress made by the shop would be unacceptable to her friend.

She was startled when she heard Violet sigh.

"Sir," Violet began, her lips set in a line. "Who is your seamstress?"

The bearded man looked at Elsa, who recovered in time to give him a nod.

"Vhy Mrs. Benson, my assistant of whom I spoke."

With a sad smile, Violet said, "I've made ladies clothes for four years, and this is the worst seam I've ever seen. Even on the plantation we made better clothes than this for the other slaves."

Elsa gasped, and the man blinked his eyes. "Excuse me?"

"On the plantation. I was a slave for most of my life, which is why I'm wearing this awful boy's outfit. And my hair—that's why it's so short."

The man's mouth fell open and he leaned forward, fascinated. "You are an escaped slave from America?"

"In a way. That's why I need a dress, so's I can look for a job. But it looks like I'm gonna have to take Sarah's offer and cut up one of her dresses."

Now the man was frowning. "Vhat is wrong with the dress, miss?"

Violet's eyes filled with pity. "Well, for one thing, the cloth is dry rotted."

"I beg to differ! This dress vas completed less than two days ago. I can show you my ledger!"

"I believe you," Violet said softly. "That means your assistant has bought old cloth that some mill couldn't sell." She stood up and lifted a fold of the gored skirt for him to inspect.

"Vait," he said, waving it away. "My eyeglasses." Hurriedly, he stepped back to his desk and produced a pair of wire-rimmed spectacles from the top drawer. Pushing them up on the bridge of his nose, he blinked, then came back over to them. "Now I vill see the dress."

"The front panel of the skirt wasn't cut along the grain," explained Violet. "See how the warp lines run crooked? The sleeves are cut like that, too."

"I see, but vhy vould someone cut it the wrong vay?"

"To squeeze more dresses out of a bolt of cloth. If you don't line the pattern up with the grain, you can cut it any which way. Once someone washes this dress and it shrinks the tiniest bit, the skirt and sleeves will hang wrong until it wears out." She gave him a sympathetic look. "Which won't take long because, like I said, the cloth's dry rotted."

Handing the dress to Elsa, Violet picked up the ball gown from the stool. She examined the inside of the gown, then regretfully looked up. "The same way."

He was shaking his head, the lines around his eyes deepening. "This cannot be! My business has fallen off since I bought the shop, but I thought things vould change vhen vord spread about the fair prices. I am heading for ruin!"

He looked close to collapse, so Violet guided him to her vacant chair. "I'm sorry to bring you such bad news, sir. Maybe your other dresses are better."

"Vhy vould they be any better?" he moaned. "They all come from the same place!"

"And where would that be?" asked Violet.

He mumbled something unintelligible into his hands.

"Sir?" Elsa asked from the chair beside him.

"Yes. I am sorry." Straightening in his chair, he removed his eyeglasses and wiped his eyes with the back of his hand. "You vere asking me a question?"

Violet leaned forward. "Your assistant, Mrs. . ."

"Mrs. Benson."

"Yes. Does she buy your fabrics and hire your seamstresses?"

The old man nodded. "She does. There are no seamstresses vorking here in the shop. I vas hoping to hire them vhen my business grew. Mrs. Benson selects the styles and cloth and pieces out the vork to different vomen in their homes."

"Does she inspect the dresses before they go to the customers?"

He lifted his hands in despair. "I thought she did."

Violet opened her mouth to speak, then closed it again.

"You haff something else to ask?"

"Well, it's just. . .does Mrs. Benson give you any receipts from the mill where she buys the cloth?"

"Receipts? Of course. I haff them in my desk."

"Do you have any that you know which fabric they match?"

Easing himself out of his chair, the man went back to his desk and opened a second drawer. Violet stood next to him as he brought out a flat wooden box and set it on top of the desk. "They are all here. Vhat do you vish to see?"

"Let's try this blue India muslin. You bought four bolts two weeks ago. That should make about eight dresses."

"Ya, that is correct."

"Do you still have the cloth in the back?"

He pursed his lips thoughtfully. "If I am not mistaken, ve haff not sent out any of the cloth you mention. Vait here.

I shall bring it out."

"One bolt will be enough," Violet called after him.

As soon as he was gone, Elsa was at Violet's side. "Do you think his assistant is cheatin' him?"

A weary smile came to her brown face. "Looks like it."

"But how?"

"By being partners with someone at one of the textile mills—buying cheap, flawed cloth, and getting a receipt that shows a much higher price. They split the difference."

"How do you know he paid too much?" Elsa picked up one of the receipts. "It ain't American money."

"True," answered Violet. "But the cloth is no good, and only untrained seamstresses could have produced such shabby work. They probably worked for next to nothing, too. This assistant is either crooked or just plain ignorant."

The man returned with a bolt of blue cloth in his arms. "Please look at this," he said anxiously, placing it on top of his desk.

"Wait, sir." Elsa reached for an ink bottle on the desk. "Wouldn't do to get ink all over everything."

"Vhy not?" muttered the old man. "Nobody is going to buy this anyway. I had such hopes that vord-of-mouth vould build my business. I fear that it is doing the opposite!"

He watched intently as Violet unwrapped a yard of fabric from the bolt. She looked up at him and sighed.

"Vhat is wrong?"

"Sir, I wish we'd never come here," she answered heavily, holding the cloth close to his face. "See if you can make a hole in the cloth by pressing it with your finger. You should only be able to do that with lace or gauze, never muslin."

Doing as she instructed, the man looked horrified at his finger protruding through the tear in the fabric. "I...I must sit down."

Elsa pulled out the desk chair while Violet helped him into it.

"See if there's some water in the back somewhere," Violet whispered.

In back of the curtain, Elsa found a roomy storeroom laden with shelves. A metal bucket sat on a small wooden table. She took the dipper from a hook on the wall, filled it with water, and brought it back into the shop.

"Here, drink this," she said soothingly, holding the dipper to the man's mouth.

He took the dipper from her hands, drained it, then handed it back to her. "Thank you, child," he whispered. He sat up. "Now I must go."

Violet and Elsa exchanged looks of alarm. "Go where?" asked Violet.

"Vhat does it matter?" he cried, sinking back into his chair. "I am ruined!"

"Now, now," consoled Violet. She patted him on the shoulder and breathed a quick prayer for wisdom. "Can't you start again, fresh? I mean, you still have this nice shop."

He shook his head. "Ve invested everything I saved for thirty years, vorking in the shipyard. I promised Anna vhen ve came here that one day she vould haff a dress shop."

"Anna?"

A smile touched his face. "Anna, my beautiful vife. She vas a genius for creating beautiful dresses. She dreamed of having a dress shop, but it vas impossible for us to do such a thing in Poland." He looked at the two girls. "Ve are Jewish, you see."

"Your wife," Violet began gently. "Is she. . .?"

"Gone, last year—soon after I purchased this place. It vas Anna who put these pictures on the valls," he said, feebly waving a hand.

His voice fell to a whisper. "Her heart, the doctor said. One morning it refused to beat, and my dear Anna left me. Forty-six years ve vere married. No children, which grieved her so. I think that is vhy she put so much energy into creating things. Our garden vas the most beautiful in Ketrzyn, and I haff already told you about the dresses she could make. She vas to be the seamstress here, and vhen ve could afford it ve vere going to hire some others that she could train. . .maybe buy another shop as vell."

"How'd you come to hire Mrs. Benson?" asked Elsa.

"One of the fabric suppliers heard about the loss of my beautiful Anna and said that he knew a good seamstress who could help me operate the business. I know nothing of clothing, but I had to try to make the shop successful— something that Anna vould haff been proud of."

Violet's eyes narrowed. "This fabric supplier. Is his mill the one on the receipts?"

"Yes, all of them. Vhy?"

"I think they cheated you, figuring that you wouldn't realize what they were doing."

"So vhat am I to do?" he moaned, clasping his hands. "I am too old to find vork anywhere and haff only a little money left."

"I have some money," said Violet.

Elsa's head shot up. "What?"

"We can find another mill," Violet was saying to the

man. "We can buy enough cloth to get started and hire someone I can train."

"Are you vishing to buy this shop from me?"

"No, sir. I'm talking about us becoming partners."

"Partners?"

"We'd have to contact every customer you've had since you opened," said Violet. Her voice filled with excitement. "Could you do that?"

"I haff their names in my ledger. None haff ever returned," he added sadly.

"We could send a letter to every one of them explaining that we are starting over and will replace every dress that was bought here if the owner wasn't satisfied."

"But how could ve afford to do such a thing?"

Violet nodded. "It'll be hard, but we'll have to do right by them if we're ever gonna get a good reputation. You said business was falling off. We've got to have the customers' good will, or one day we'll have nothing.

"We could tell them that it'll take some time," Violet continued. "For every dress that we sell to a new customer, we'll give one to a customer who has returned a faulty dress. Hopefully, we'll get some new customers when we advertise."

The man tilted his head thoughtfully. "Perhaps ve vould need to hire two more seamstresses. The little that I haff put aside would take care of this until ve started making a profit. You mentioned advertising?"

"In the newspaper. And of course we'll need a sign."

"I already haff a sign. A beautiful one, carved from mahogany."

"You do?" asked Elsa. "Why ain't it over the door?"

"Because it says Anna's Quality Ladies' Clothiers. I

never could bring myself to use it after she died. Now I am glad that I did not because it vould haff been untrue."

Violet smiled. "If you take me on as a partner, you'll be proud to put Anna's name over the shop. What do you think?"

The man hesitated. "Vhy do you vant to go into business with me?" he asked, studying her face. "You don't even know my name. And I don't know you."

"My name is Violet Bowman, and I can give you references as to my honesty. You'll have to take my word for my sewing ability, but since I'm investing every penny that I have, it doesn't make sense that I'd plan to fail."

"No, it doesn't," he agreed. A slow smile spread across his face. "I belief you! You and I vill be partners, Miss Violet." Standing, he took her hand. "And I think I vill bless the day that you came into my shop."

"So will I," agreed Violet. "By the way, what is your name?"

The man chuckled. "Jacob. Jacob Zalyski. Vhere do you liff, Miss Violet?"

She glanced at Elsa and smiled. "I'm staying with dear friends at the Palmer House Inn, but I'll be lookin' for a room to rent now."

"How are you gonna pay for a room if all your money is invested in the shop?" asked Elsa.

Worry came to Jacob's eyes. "I haff only the small flat upstairs, vhere I live." After a second, he brightened. "Perhaps ve could curtain off part of the storage room and put a small bed and chest there, until ve can afford to rent you a place? After all, ve haff more than enough useless fabric to make curtains."

"That won't do," Violet answered. "I'd like to stay here

at the shop because I'm gonna be sewing from morning 'til night until we get caught up. But we'll need the extra space in there to do the work."

Elsa glanced around the shop. "Why not take your sewing out here?"

"Here?"

"In that corner over there." She pointed to her left. "There's room for a couple sewing tables and some stools. I think it'd be interesting to people passing by to see the work bein' done."

Folding her arms, Violet walked over to the area of the shop Elsa had pointed out and slowly turned around. "It might draw some customers." She looked over at Jacob. "What do you think, sir?"

"That is good," he answered with a nod.

Violet looked around again. "We'd have room for some racks, but do you think it would disturb customers to see a Negro working here?"

Raising his eyebrows, Jacob said, "Vhy should it disturb them? I am sure they haff seen Negroes vorking before."

Her head snapped up. "Here in Bristol?"

"Yes. I vorked vith some Negro men in the shipyards."

"And women and children—have you seen any?"

"I haff seen some dark-skinned children in town, and there is a woman who cooks at Christopher's, a restaurant not far from here."

Violet closed her eyes, overwhelmed by the good things that had happened so quickly. *I'm a partner in a business, I have a place to stay, and there are others here who look like me.* Opening her eyes, she smiled at the blurred images of Elsa and Jacob. *Thank You, Father,* she whispered under her breath.

# eight

David left after breakfast the next morning to make some business calls, giving Sarah a hurried kiss at the door. Violet had disappeared earlier, having explained the night before that she would be helping Jacob get the shop ready.

"I might not be here tonight if we get the sleeping area set up," she'd said. Her face had been a mixture of regret at leaving her friends and eagerness to get started at her new business. "But I'll come by before you leave for Miss Martin's, and I'll see you before you go back to Charleston."

Sarah understood. Her dear friend would have to devote herself almost completely to the business if it were to succeed. She and David had become alarmed, though, when Violet told them about her planned living arrangements. David offered to give her some money to find a proper place. "You'll get sick sleeping in a drafty old storage room," he'd warned.

Violet would hear nothing of it. She'd thanked him, but said, "It's not drafty, and I need to be close to my work if we're ever gonna make the business a success."

*That's my friend, independent as the day is long!* thought Sarah as she sat on the side of her bed, dressing Eileen.

Elsa's knock sounded at her door. After breakfast she'd asked permission to check on her new-found friend Danny, the boy who washed windows. "Come in," Sarah called softly.

The girl walked in and smiled when the baby began chattering at her. "Good mornin', Eileen," Elsa cooed back. "Did you sleep good?"

"She slept all night," Sarah answered for her daughter, "and I'm glad. Did you find the boy?" Elsa had told her about how the younger children had frightened Danny, and she was proud of the girl for taking up for him.

"Yes, ma'am. He's out back sweepin' off the benches. Can I help you with anything, Miss Sarah?"

"My husband won't be back until this afternoon," Sarah told her while her fingers fastened the tiny buttons at the back of Eileen's gown. "I'd like you to go walking with Eileen and me, then perhaps later we'll buy some sandwiches and bring them to Violet's shop for lunch. We could have a picnic there, if the baby doesn't get too fussy for her nap."

"That'd be fun," agreed Elsa, her eyes sparkling. "It's nice and cool outside, so you might want to bring a little shawl for Eileen here." She picked up the pair of white kid slippers from the edge of the bed and got down on her knees to tie them on the baby's feet.

After the baby was dressed, Sarah combed her own hair and fastened it at the nape of her neck with a ribbon, then covered it with a green silk capote hat to match her green calico dress. Elsa, hatless in her favorite blue dress, found a knit shawl to tuck into Eileen's pram stored behind the staircase in the lobby.

"Where are we going?" asked Elsa when they'd left the hotel, still not able to believe that she, Elsa Stubbs, was out strolling like a proper English lady.

Sarah didn't answer for a minute. Finally she said, "The

steward gave me directions to a house I'd like to see."

"Yes, ma'am," answered Elsa. "I saw a couple pretty ones yesterday when I went shopping with Violet. I think flower boxes are so nice!"

"They are." Sarah was quiet, pushing Eileen's pram along the cobblestones, worn smooth by a century of carriages and sledges. Twenty minutes later they were out of the business district and on Colleton Road, lined with shaded Georgian houses. A half-mile farther, the road came to a dead end at the stone walls of a rambling estate.

Through the wrought-iron gate could be seen a house of warm red brick with a white-painted Regency porch. A circular lily-pond in front sparkled in the sunlight, and the green beds of shrubs lining the brick walkway were neatly manicured. Two gardeners were the only signs of life— one raked the gravel carriage-way, while the other pulled weeds from a flower bed.

"Hadenwilde Manor," Sarah said, her tone flat and her face expressionless. "I was born here."

"You was?" Elsa's eyes grew wide. "In *this* house?"

"In the servants' quarters. My mother was the cook."

"What about your daddy?" the girl asked without thinking.

Sarah's face clouded. "I haven't any idea who my father is. Just someone who. . .hid in an alley and forced himself on my poor mother when she was going to visit some friends."

"Oh, Miss Sarah, I'm so sorry!"

Seeming not to hear, Sarah murmured, "She was beautiful. And she would sing to me every night when work was finished. The Nortons, who live here, wouldn't give her any days off after I was born—punishment for having a child without being married. Oh, they claimed they were doing her a favor because no one else would want to hire her, but. . . ."

Her lips tightened. Then she went on. "They cut her wages in half, too. Later they fired her when Celly hid the doll under my bed."

"Celly?"

"A maid who worked here. I've asked myself hundreds of times why she did it, but I'll never understand why."

Elsa blinked. "Hid a doll?"

Nodding slightly, Sarah said, "Elizabeth's doll. Elizabeth was Mrs. Norton's daughter."

"And that maid—Celly? She put it under your bed to get your mother fired?"

"I still don't understand why. It worked, too. Mrs. Norton refused to give us references, and she told her friends that we were dishonest. Nobody would see us— except Mrs. Gerty."

Elsa put her clenched fists on her hips, wishing she had a cannon aimed at the brick house, like the one in *The Hidden Patriot*, one of the books she'd read. "Well, it's a good thing Mrs. Gerty didn't listen to that gossip!"

Sarah turned to her, an attempt at a smile on her face though her eyes were wet with tears. "Don't be angry, Elsa. I forgave them a long time ago—or so I thought. I should never have come here because it stirred up the old hatreds." She sighed. "Especially for Mrs. Gerty."

"But you said she hired you—"

"But not my mother. Mrs. Gerty wanted only children, except for her housekeeper and cook. You can pay children a pittance, you see, and you can scare them, too. She liked to scare us, threatening to put me in the cellar with the rats if I didn't work harder."

Sarah's words were rushed. She seemed to be anxious to get them all out. "She never gave me a day off—not even when my mother died from pneumonia after working in a textile mill."

Elsa gasped, putting a hand on Sarah's arm. "And you just a little girl!"

Sarah reached for a handkerchief in her beaded bag and wiped her eyes. "I'm sorry, Elsa. Here I am, saying all kinds of things that I shouldn't say. I just wish. . . ."

"Yes, ma'am?"

"I wish I could knock on that door and tell Mrs. Norton that I never touched that doll, and that if she hadn't fired her, my mother might still be alive and cooking for her today."

"She never found out that you didn't do it?"

"My mother heard from one of the other servants that Celly, the girl who hid the doll under my bed, admitted it and was fired. Mother came back here to ask for her job back, but Mrs. Norton wouldn't see her."

Elsa's eyes narrowed into slits as she watched the house in front of her. "Why don't we march up to that front door? I'll go with you!" She was surprised to hear herself talk, and even more surprised to know that she meant every word. What had happened to the frightened little girl who quaked every time someone sent her a harsh look?

Sarah smiled. "Wouldn't that be something?"

"I'd like to see the look on her face when she sees what a fine lady you are now!"

Picking up Eileen, who was attempting to climb out of her pram, Sarah hugged her tightly. "Time mellows people, sometimes," she said, looking at Elsa over the baby's head. "For all I know, Mrs. Norton has regretted everything that happened back then."

Elsa shook her head doubtfully. "I don't know. Some people want to believe the worst about others, and nothin' can make them change their minds. Time seems to make folks like that worse."

Sarah put Eileen back in the pram, then turned it around. "Let's go," she told Elsa. "I shouldn't have come here."

They walked along without speaking, ignoring the sights and sounds around them. Sarah fought against bitterness, which like a fist was gripping her heart.

*Lord, I thought I forgave them,* she prayed. *But it hurts so much to think about what they did to my mother. Please give me the grace to forgive them again.*

She noticed that the girl at her side still had a frown on her face. *I've infected Elsa with my bitterness too. . .or perhaps she has some bitter thoughts of her own. There's no telling what she's been through.*

Sarah cleared her throat. "When you said time makes some people worse, who were you talking about?"

"Why, that Mrs. Norton woman," said Elsa.

"But you were thinking about someone else, weren't you?"

The girl nodded. "My Aunt Hattie."

"The one who raised you?"

"Yes, ma'am. I loved her because she was all I had by way of family. But she must'a told me every day that I was goin' to turn out like my daddy. Trash, was what she called us."

"Do you believe that?"

Elsa raised her eyebrows. "That I'm trash? I used to believe it. But I been wondering lately if she was wrong."

Eileen was trying to climb out of the moving pram, and Elsa stepped forward to take her in her arms. "I'll just carry her, if you don't mind," she told Sarah.

When they'd walked a bit, Sarah, pushing the empty pram, asked, "What made you start wondering about your aunt being wrong?"

Elsa gave her an affectionate smile. "Miss Sarah, you had a lot to do with it. You and Mr. David."

"Really?" Sarah returned her smile. "How so?"

"By treatin' me like I was smart. And by trusting me with Eileen, here. But you know what helped the most?"

"Tell me."

"Me," echoed Eileen, twisting a lock of Elsa's hair around her finger.

Elsa grinned at the baby. "When Violet showed me how to be saved. If Jesus is my Savior, then I must be worth somethin' because of Him, even if I am a servant."

"It's amazing that you could change your thinking so quickly!" said Sarah. "It took me years to believe I had any right to be born."

"Oh, I still have some bad thoughts," confessed Elsa. "I can hear my aunt calling me stupid and ugly sometimes. Or Mrs. Clark tellin' me how worthless I am." Hesitating briefly, she added, "Back there at the house, when you said you'd forgiven those people once. How'd you do that?"

"It didn't come easy, and I realize now that I've got some of those hard feelings left. It's natural to hate someone who has hurt you. But do you know why I *must* forgive them? And why you must forgive your aunt and Mrs. Clark?"

Elsa nodded. "Violet explained it to me, and I read it in her Bible on ship. God wants us to."

"Too," repeated Eileen, enjoying her perch in Elsa's arms.

Sarah and Elsa exchanged glances and laughed. "That's right," Sarah finally said. "When I think about how Jesus forgave those who put Him on the cross, I feel ashamed of my bitterness."

"You're right. I been thinking about forgiving them, I'm just not sure how to go about it."

"Ask God to help you forgive them and He will. I'm going to have to ask the same thing tonight—would you like for us to pray together?"

"You mean that, ma'am?"

"I do."

"Do," echoed Eileen.

Violet was seated in an armchair with a dress across her lap when they walked in the shop. "Well, glory be!" she exclaimed, setting the dress on the nearby stool.

Elsa's eyes were wide. "You got a customer already?"

"This is that chambray dress that we can't sell. Jacob and I realized this morning that I'm gonna need something else to wear as soon as possible. I'm cutting this down to fit, and hopefully it'll last long enough for me to sew a better one." She embraced Sarah and gave Eileen a hug.

Sarah held out a good-sized brown paper parcel. "Here are some sandwiches and fruit for lunch."

"How thoughtful!" Violet said as she reached for the parcel. "Feels like there's a lot of food in here. Can you stay and share it?"

"That's what we planned. We brought enough for your friend Jacob too. Is he here?"

Violet's smile faded. "He's gone to tell Mrs. Benson that

she's fired. He was nervous when he left here, and I've been praying as I worked that everything would go all right."

Smiling again, she handed the parcel back to Sarah. "Please hold this while I find something for us to spread out and sit on. At least we'll find another use for some of the cloth we have in the back. And if Jacob doesn't show up, we can save some food for him, if you don't mind."

She came back through the curtained doorway with a folded piece of blue and white striped cotton. Flapping it open, she spread it out on the wooden floor. "I've got the rugs hanging out back to air out," she said as they sat down. "They had a bit of a musty smell."

"You mentioned having a lot of useless cloth in the store-room," Sarah said, handing out sandwiches of roast beef on soft brown bread. "What are you planning to do with it?"

Violet shrugged. "Throw it away, I suppose. We can't use it."

"That's a shame!" exclaimed Elsa. She began tearing Eileen's sandwich into manageable pieces. "To cheat that man like they did!"

"Isn't there anything you can do to recover some of that loss?" asked Sarah.

"I don't think so. Jacob is afraid of causing trouble. I think he has bad memories of the police back in Poland. And I sure can't sashay down to the mill and demand they give us some good fabric." She sighed. "It sure would help, though, if we didn't have to spend so much on replacing the rotten stuff they sold Jacob."

Sarah was thoughtful as she watched Eileen pick up bits of food with her fingers. "You know," she finally said,

"David uses a lawyer here in Bristol to draw up shipping contracts. I wonder if he could do anything?"

"Jacob and I talked about hiring a lawyer," Violet said. "I appreciate your offer, but we don't want to do that."

"Why?" asked Elsa.

"Because we don't know how powerful the owner of this mill is. It wouldn't do to have the shop accidentally burn down or something like that."

Elsa frowned. "But you ain't even sure if the owner knows about it. Didn't Mr. Jacob say it was a vendor who told him about Mrs. Benson?"

"Yes."

"Then it must'a been the same man who sold the cloth. What if he's doing it to other people, too? People he figures won't complain."

Violet threw her hands up helplessly. "I don't know. I've got to respect Jacob's wishes not to involve the law or any lawyers." Changing the subject, she said, "This is so nice. It was sure good of you to think about me."

"We love you," Sarah told her with a sad smile. "And I'm going to hate it when we have to go back to Charleston and leave you here."

Closing her eyes, Violet nodded. "I don't want to think about that now. Please come see me before you do."

"You know that we will. And we'll be praying that this shop is a huge success!"


Celly watched the front of the hotel from the shadowy overhang of the wheelwright's shop down the street. *They've gotta either come or go sometime,* she thought, yawning. *I should'a woke up and gotten here earlier.* It had been hard enough to get up at eleven after working all night.

*That's all right. Won't be long 'til I won't have to work at all!*

The owner of the shop, a nervous-looking man with auburn hair and mutton-chop whiskers, came outside after she'd been on his stoop for an hour. "Need some help ma'am?" Hands clasped together tightly, his expression was one of worried distaste.

Celly gave him her brightest smile. "Oh, sir," she said with eyelashes fluttering. "I'm watching for the ladies in my church benevolence society. We're gonna bring some doilies we've crocheted to the poor people down in the slums. Do you mind if I wait here just a little longer?"

After a confused glance at Celly's revealing neckline and tight bodice, the man began to retreat. "Um, yes. All right."

Celly smiled to herself after the man was back in his shop. *He knows what I am but he's scared to say anything. Scared I'll cause a scene.*

Her diligence was rewarded ten minutes later with the sight of a familiar face coming down the street. *Sarah Brown!* she thought. There was someone with her, a tall girl pushing a pram while Sarah held the baby.

Her sister? She didn't remember that Sarah had any family beside her mother. *Must be a servant,* she thought. *If Sarah was as wealthy as she looked, she must have loads of servants.*

Celly had gotten the answer she'd come for. If Sarah had time to take a stroll in town, she and her husband wouldn't be checking out of the hotel right away. *And my dress will be ready tomorrow!*

Back in the hotel suite that night, David listened intently to Sarah's account of her lunch with Violet. Having just put Eileen to bed, they were in the sitting room on two chairs pulled up to an open window.

"I wish she'd let me talk with James Pevey," he said. "He's a first-rate lawyer, and I believe he could get the mill owner to make amends without involving the law."

"But Violet asked us not to. We can't go against that."

"I know, but it frustrates me to see someone taken advantage of."

"Me too," sighed Sarah. "You should have seen Elsa's face when we talked about it at lunch. She'd storm down to that mill herself if we let her."

David smiled. "Whatever happened to the shy mouse who used to slip around the house on tiptoe?"

"Gone forever, I hope. I like this Elsa better. She's got spirit."

"Where is she now, by the way?"

"She promised the boy who works here, Danny, that she'd teach him how to play Whist whenever his chores were finished."

David nodded absently, his brow furrowed.

When he didn't speak for a few seconds, Sarah reached over and tapped him on the arm. "What are you thinking about?"

"What you said. About Elsa storming over to the mill."

Sarah's eyebrows shot up. "Surely you're not. . ."

"Of course not," he said, holding up a hand. "But why can't you and I pay a friendly visit on the mill's owner?"

"Because Violet said she and Jacob don't want any trouble."

"I don't think there will be. Surely no business owner

who wants to continue doing business is going to risk ruining his reputation by selling inferior cloth."

Sarah nodded. "We figure that it's an employee. But when I mentioned hiring a lawyer, Violet asked me not to."

"Did she forbid you and me from talking with the owner?"

Sarah shifted uneasily in her chair. "Well, no."

"Then what can it harm?"

"Their shop, for one thing. She mentioned someone getting angry enough to burn it down."

"I don't think that's going to happen."

"But how can you be sure?"

David shook his head. "I can't be, of course. But, say it does. God has blessed us with a more than comfortable living these past few years. If something happens to the shop, we'll help Violet and her partner get started somewhere else. Bristol's not the only city in England."

From her chair Sarah watched her husband's face. *He has a way with people,* she thought. *That's why he's been so successful in business lately—people can tell he's honest and hard working. He could probably talk the mill owner into setting things right. But what about Violet? She didn't want—*

"Well?" asked David, interrupting her thoughts. "What do you think?"

"I guess it'd be all right," she said with uncertainty.

He smiled at her reluctance. "We can still send Elsa."

Sarah smiled back. "When do you want to go?"

"I've got business in the morning. How about after lunch?"

"That's good. Eileen can stay here with Elsa."

## nine

*Perfect!* thought Celly, peering in the cracked mirror over her dresser as she arranged the veiled hat on her head. Her mass of scarlet hair was pinned up severely. The pink in her scarred cheeks was not from sunshine—which until recently she had had little acquaintance with—but from the tightness of the high collar.

*I hope I won't have to wear this too long.* She tugged at the collar, unsuccessfully trying to stretch some ease into the tightly woven fabric.

A half-full bottle of gin and a rock-hard wedge of yellow cheese sat on the table. Celly pulled the cork from the bottle and took a couple swigs. Why hadn't Raymond thought to take the bottle with him when he disappeared? He hadn't been there when she got home that morning. *He's either runnin' from his gamblin' partners, or he's at the bottom of the Avon.* In any event, Raymond's whereabouts weren't her problem. She had more important things to think about.

Violet peered through the plate glass window of Christopher's, a bakery and tea room on Elgin Road, wondering if she dared walk inside. The breakfast crowd had thinned to a handful of people who were finishing up their meals.

Standing back, Violet caught her reflection in the glass. *It feels so nice to look feminine again,* she thought, smoothing the folds of the dress she'd cut down the day

101

before. A new Dunstable straw bonnet covered most of her short hair, and she'd splurged on a tiny bottle of Rose Petal, dabbed behind her ears.

She felt a little guilty for not being at work in the shop, but she'd gotten up at four and had already put in a good six hours. *I've got to see for myself!*

Taking a deep breath for courage, Violet straightened her shoulders and walked into the restaurant. A waiter carrying a pastry tray noticed her immediately. "May I help you?"

Violet cleared her throat. "Yes, please. I've been told that you have a Negro cook employed here."

The man nodded and jerked his head toward a swinging door at the back. "Deborah."

Without saying another word, the waiter carried his tray to a corner table. Violet assumed this meant she was welcome to go into the kitchen. Still, when she got to the door, she knocked.

"Come in!" called a voice from the other side.

Violet's heart seemed to beat in her throat as she gave the door a tentative push. She entered a good-sized kitchen, stuffy with the heat from its massive oven. Violet's eyes landed on a heavy-set woman kneading a mound of dough on a wooden table.

The woman looked surprised, but smiled as Violet approached. "I'm sorry," she said with a precise British accent. "We haven't any openings right now."

Violet shook her head. "I'm not lookin' for a job. I just wanted to see you."

"Me? Why?"

"Because I just came here from the United States, and I can't ever go back, and I was so worried that I'd be the only Negro in England." To Violet's embarrassment, she was unable to stop the torrent of words that rushed out. "My business partner, Mr. Zalyski, told me he'd seen you here and that he's seen other Negroes, too, and I couldn't wait 'til I saw you for myself." Taking a deep breath, she added, "I'm Violet Bowman."

The woman laughed, a deep, musical sound. "Deborah Turnley is mine. I'd shake your hand, but as you can see. ..." She held up flour-covered hands before plunging them back into the dough.

"How did you come to live here?"

"Why, I was born here—as were my mother and father."

"How did they come to be born in England?"

Her eyes crinkling at the corners, Deborah said, "My grandparents got invited here by the slave traders."

Violet's mouth fell open. "England had slavery?"

"Once upon a time. But it was abolished when I was a girl." She studied her visitor. "Were you a slave?"

"My master set me free four years ago."

"Then if you're free, why can't you go back to the States?"

"Because I helped some runaways."

Deborah's face grew sympathetic. "So you've become a stranger in a strange land, haven't you?"

"Why, that's from the Bible!" exclaimed Violet. "Are you a believer?"

"Saved by grace and washed in the blood of the Lamb! How about you?"

"Since I was a girl. Do you have a church?"

"Mr. Lowden, one of our customers here, lets us use his old carriage house for services." She grinned. "I'll bet you wouldn't be disappointed if I invited you."

"I can hardly contain my joy!" said Violet. She listened to the woman's directions to the meeting place and realized it was only three blocks away from the clothing shop. *God is surely in this!* she thought.

Reluctantly, Violet said good-bye to Deborah so that they could both return to their work. She was about to leave when a question came to mind. She looked back at her new friend. "I was just wondering. . .these church services. Are there any other Negroes who attend?"

Chuckling, Deborah said, "Child, everyone there will be of the dark-skinned race. You and I aren't the only Negroes in England."


"What's the matter, Eileen?" Elsa picked up the baby's doll from where she'd thrown it on the floor. "Don't you want to play?"

"Ow," Eileen said for the third time, pointing to a window.

"You want to see what's outside?"

Eileen toddled over to the window and stretched on her bare toes, trying to reach the glass. She turned an imploring look to Elsa. "Ow?"

"Well, all right, let's look at what's goin' on," said Elsa. Setting the doll down, she walked over to the little girl and lifted her in her arms. "See?" she said, turning her toward the glass.

Instead of calming down, Eileen grew more agitated and pointed to the street below. "Go ow!"

"We can't do that, sweetheart. It's about time for your nap."

Eileen shook her head and pointed again. "Go ow!" She put a chubby hand up to Elsa's cheek and leaned her head forward so their faces almost touched. "Esa?"

Elsa smiled. "Are you trying to say Elsa?"

"Go ow?"

Sighing, Elsa nodded. "All right. But just for a little while. Then you've got to take a nap."

After changing Eileen's diaper and slipping some stockings over her bare feet, Elsa picked the baby up and started for the door. "You're goin' to have to ride in your pram," she said with gentle sternness. "It ain't safe for me to be carrying you around like this. If I trip or something you could get hurt."

Eileen gave her an uncomprehending look. Once they were out in the hall, she gave a sharp squeal and tightened her grip around Elsa's neck.

"What's wrong?" Elsa asked.

The baby, trembling and clinging even tighter, was staring at a figure standing at the end of the hallway.

"It's all right," Elsa whispered, patting Eileen on the back. "It's just a lady." She could understand the baby's fear, however, because the lady was dressed in black from head to toe, with a dark veil covering her face. *A widow,* she thought. Elsa gave the woman a compassionate smile as they turned down the corridor and passed her. The lady returned her acknowledgment with a slight nod.

Joseph Gilliatt sat back in his leather chair, his hands steepled on the desk before him. Tired eyes revealed anger just below their surface. When he finally spoke, his voice was surprisingly soft.

"Your friend still has the receipts?"

Sarah, who'd let David do the initial explaining, sat up in her chair. "Our maid, Elsa, saw the receipts. That's how we knew your mill sold the cloth."

Mr. Gilliatt nodded his gray head. "I'm afraid I know what has happened, and I'm deeply sorry for it."

Lifting his eyebrows, David said, "Do you mind telling us?"

"Not at all. I bought another, much smaller mill a couple years ago. It was a family-type operation, and when the head of the family died, the business failed. I didn't need the mill, but I figured one day we'd expand. The building was in a good location."

"Are you saying that the cloth came from that mill?"

"Yes," answered the man. "And there's no telling how long it sat in their storage room before I bought the business. I didn't know what shape the cloth was in, but I only sell quality fabric. I told Mr. Yates, my representative, to give the material to any charities that could put it to use. I'm afraid that's what he sold Mr. Zalyski and no telling who else. I've had some trouble with him before, and it's only because he's a distant cousin that I didn't fire him then. This time, I won't be so forgiving."

"But why would he sell bad cloth?" asked Sarah.

The man gave her a weary smile. "One hundred percent profit, my dear. Many a man has sold his principals for much less."

David's face was hopeful. "Can you help Mr. Zalyski?"

"Of course. Today, in fact. I'll send someone to his shop to inventory the receipts and replace every yard he bought from me." He held up a hand to forestall their thanks. "Also, to make meager amends for the damage done to the shop's reputation, I'll add two hundred yards of my finest weaves."

Overcome with emotion, Sarah reached across the desk

and covered his spotted hand with her gloved one. "You are a good man, sir," she said, her voice wavering.

The man looked away and blinked his eyes. "I have a reputation for being ruthless. Few people call me good."

"Well, I think you are."

Mr. Gilliatt blinked his eyes again. "I believe I'll change that to three hundred yards."

Danny shifted the heavy rolled carpet to his other shoulder as he climbed the steps of the service staircase. He moved slowly, not having a free hand for the railing. Halfway between the first and second floor, he heard the door on the landing above him open and close. *Must be George,* he thought. It was time to pick up trays from customers who had lunched in their rooms.

Seconds later, he was startled to find a woman dressed in black coming down the stairs toward him. He wondered if she realized she was on the servants' stairway. "Are you lost?" he asked.

The woman shook her head and continued to descend, passing him with quick steps.

He wondered if she'd heard him. Turning, he watched her retreating back and debated whether he should tell her she was on the wrong staircase. He didn't want to make her angry. Maybe it was all right, even though she wasn't a servant.

Just before the woman got to the bottom landing, Danny noticed a bit of red hair coiled beneath the hat. His face broke into a grin. "Miss Celly?" he called out.

The woman froze. Then she moved again, quicker than before, and disappeared through the first floor doorway.

Elsa stopped in front of a toy shop to peer through its elaborately timbered glass window. Toys were something new to her—even Eileen's small collection of dolls and carved animals fascinated her immensely.

Oblivious to the people bustling past her, Elsa stood mesmerized by the colorful merchandise. The display held more toys than she'd ever seen in one place. Hobby-horses, jigsaw puzzles, music boxes, kites, tin soldiers, and whistles sat in enticing profusion before a backdrop of cheery red velvet.

Eileen had fallen asleep, lulled by the rocking of the pram's wheels. *She'd love this place,* thought Elsa as she leaned forward to check on the slumbering baby.

The window on the other side of the door was filled with dolls. Set amongst the dolls was a toy pram of framed navy-blue. *Just the size for Eileen's rag doll,* she thought, admiring the roses painted on each side and the glossy black metal wheels.

She pictured the delight on the little girl's face while pushing her rag doll around the hotel room. It might make her like her own pram a little better. Elsa's hand went down to the crochet bag on her arm. She wasn't sure of the English money system, but certainly she had enough coins to buy the toy.

Glancing down at the sleeping child, she wondered if she could scoop Eileen up in her arms without waking her. "Likely not," she murmured. She'd seen enough prams waiting outside various shops to know that they weren't welcome inside. She sighed, eyeing the toy again before pushing the pram away from the shop window.

*I'll have to come back later. But what if it gets sold? Was it the only one in the shop?* Again, Elsa imagined Eileen toddling behind the toy pram. *I know she'd love it!*

A millinery shop was just ahead. Elsa noticed a pram waiting outside the store. Taking a couple steps closer, she realized that a sleeping baby was inside the pram.

She looked back at the toy store with longing. *I'd only be inside a few minutes, and I could keep an eye on her through the door.*

"Would you like to stop by Violet's and tell her the news?" asked David.

"Could we?"

He laughed. "Don't pretend you weren't thinking about it."

Smiling back at her husband, Sarah squeezed his arm. "You know me too well."

"Would you like to go to a nice restaurant afterward? I've got a hankering for seafood."

"That would be nice, but what about Elsa and the baby?"

"I told Elsa that she should order supper sent up to them." David grinned sheepishly. "I was hoping we could spend the whole afternoon together."

Sarah raised her eyebrows in mock suspicion. "So you plotted with Elsa, did you?"

"Are you mad?"

"Terribly."

Feigning disappointment, David pointed to a bookstore. "What if I bought you a book—would that put me back in your good graces?"

Sarah smiled. "It wouldn't hurt."

"Shall I wrap your purchase, Miss?" asked the shop-keeper at the toy store, a middle-aged woman with a friendly smile.

Elsa glanced back at the door. "Well. . ."

"It'll only take a second. Keeps the dust off, you see."

"All right—thank you."

Five minutes later, Elsa tucked the brown-paper parcel under her arm and headed for the door. *I'll let her tear the wrappings off soon as we get back to the hotel, if she's awake.*

It was going to be awkward, pushing the pram with one hand, but the hotel was only a block away. Elsa had just reached for the handle when it dawned on her that the pram was empty.

"Eileen?" Leaning forward, Elsa's face drained of color. The package under her arm fell to the sidewalk with a crunch. Frantically, she scanned the sidewalk. Finding no sign of Eileen, she grabbed the arm of a young man passing by.

"A baby girl—have you seen her?"

The man shook his head and walked away. Two women, obviously mother and daughter, came out of the shop next door and turned puzzled expressions toward Elsa. She ran over to them. "Please," she said, sobbing. "The baby's not in her pram! Have you seen her?"

The older woman took one glance at the empty pram and said, "You mean your baby's missing?"

"Not my baby! But I was tending to her and she's gone!" Tears streamed down Elsa's cheeks. "Please help me find her!"

"Calm down," ordered the older woman, putting an arm around Elsa's shoulder. A crowd had gathered, drawn by the commotion.

The woman turned to her daughter. "Go find a policeman."

## ten

Two blue-coated policemen were standing outside the hotel that evening when David and Sarah arrived. One stepped forward and took off his hat. "Would you be Mr. and Mrs. Adams?"

"Yes," answered David, his brow furrowed. "What do you—"

"Eileen and Elsa," cut in Sarah, her hand on her heart. "Has something happened?"

The man did not answer at once, and David grew alarmed when he spotted the tears rimming his eyes. "Sir, please tell us what is wrong!" he begged.

"Your child, sir. She's missing."

*I should'a been a coachman,* Celly thought, smiling to herself as she held tightly to the reins of the hired cart. She glanced up at the murky sky and hoped she'd make it to the outland before the sun set completely. Not that she was afraid of darkness, but she couldn't have the horse stumble and break a leg.

There was no sound, save horse hooves and wheels against the rutted dirt road. The child, lying among rags in the back, was quiet and would be so for hours. A good dose of rum mixed with honey-water had taken care of that.

Just before the sky turned to ink, Celly pulled the cart up in front of a crumbling stone cottage with a thatched roof. A dim glow from the encrusted window-panes told her that at least one occupant was awake.

She swung down from the wagon seat, walked round to the back, and felt around in the rags. A sluggish whimpering came from the baby as Celly lifted her into her arms. Turning, she walked over to the front door of the cottage and pulled open the door.

The woman, toothless and shapeless, hardly looked up from the table as Celly walked into the room. She lowered the mutton chop bone she'd been gumming and said, "So, you've come here with another one. I ain't keepin' any more."

Celly set Eileen down on the dirt floor. "I've had a run of bad luck, but I aim to start payin' you again."

A laugh as dry and papery as the woman's skin came from her mouth. "You ain't paid me in weeks. How do you think I manage to feed your little—"

"All that's gonna change," Celly cut in. "Here's some money." She was glad she'd worked the night before, for the woman stared greedily at the coins Celly set on the table. "There'll be more where that came from. Plenty more."

Easing up from her stool, the woman left a trail of fetid body odor as she limped over to the child. She turned to Celly in surprise. "This ain't no newborn. Where did you get it?"

Sighing, Celly looked around the room at the other sleeping children. There was no way she could pass this child off as her own—she'd just had one six months earlier, and her mother's eyes were sharper than she'd realized. "A dear friend of mine. She died yesterday, and I didn't want her baby to go to no charity home."

"So you brought her here?" Celly's mother shook her

head. "Be better off in one o' them homes. When are you gonna come get these brats? Ain't right to make me raise them. I'm too old."

"Soon, I promise. And we'll have a big house with servants, and you won't have to lift a finger." *As long as you stay out of my sight,* she added under her breath.

Celly hated to spend the night in the old shack, but it was far too dangerous to travel at night. Without a word to her mother, she curled up on a broken-down settee, hoping that no vermin would crawl on her as she slept.


"I have given your wife and the girl some laudanum," said Dr. Thompson as he walked back into the sitting room. "Now I should like for you to take some. It's late, and you need to rest."

Bleary-eyed, David shook his head. "I want to go back out and look for her. Will you stay here and take care of them?"

"But you don't know this city as well as the police. Why don't you stay here and let them do their job?"

David pulled himself up from his chair. "I have to do something." His voice cracking, he added, "She's out there somewhere, wondering why we haven't come to get her."

Dr. Thompson sighed. It had been a long day and he was tired. He had children, too, grown and married, and it would break his heart if something happened to one of them. "All right," he finally said. "I shall rest here on your sofa."


The next morning, Eileen opened her eyes and sat up. Blinking, she tried to place her surroundings. She'd lived in so many places lately. Was this another place, and were Mother and Daddy asleep in the next room?

She heard a smacking sound and looked behind her. A baby, smaller than herself, had the corner of the rag it was lying on clutched in both hands, and was frantically trying to bring it to its mouth.

Climbing to her feet, Eileen raised her gown and tugged at her sodden diaper, uncomfortably chafing against her skin. She looked around for Mother or Elsa. Maybe they were going to get her another diaper so she could be changed.

She started at the sound of footsteps outside the room. Was that Mother? The door opened and a big person walked in.

Startled, Eileen drew in a shuddering gulp of air. The big person wasn't Mother or Daddy or even Elsa. She looked scary, even more frightening than the person with the black clothes had been. At the thought of the person in black, Eileen flinched. Was she here, too? Was she going to hit her again and make her drink nasty water?

The big person had set a bucket on the table and was coming closer. "Well, you're finally up," said the person. "And ain't you a pretty one?"

Eileen began to take steps backward, until she tripped on the baby. She ended in a heap on top of the baby, who erupted in an ear-piercing squall. That was too much. Eileen opened her mouth and began to shriek. She shrieked so loudly that she couldn't hear the big person yelling at her and couldn't hear the cries of the other baby. She shrieked until her throat was raw and her body began heaving with dry sobs. Still her mother and father didn't come.

Elsa was awakened by the sound of sobs in the next room. Her thoughts were still foggy from the laudanum, so it took her a couple seconds to identify the source.

*Miss Sarah,* she remembered. *She's crying for Eileen.* So it hadn't been a nightmare. Eileen was missing . . .because of her.

Elsa closed her swollen eyes and wished that she could sleep forever. If only she'd stayed inside yesterday, if only she hadn't left the baby outside the toy store! She couldn't remember what happened to the toy pram. *I hope I never see it again!*

*Oh God,* she prayed, *Please keep Eileen safe. And please, please help us find her.* The tears flowed, dampening her pillowcase. *If something has to happen to anybody, please let it happen to me, not Eileen. Please.*

Bitterness took hold, and Elsa lifted her eyes to the ceiling. *Are you listening to me, God? I thought You cared about us! If this is how You show Your love, I'd rather go back to the way things were before.*

Panic ran through her. Had she just brought down some dreadful curse on herself? Taking shallow breaths, Elsa waited for her heart to stop beating or for the walls to fall down on her. Anything would be better than this!

She had to get up. As much as she dreaded it, she had to tell Sarah and David how sorry she was. It wouldn't bring back their baby.

The baby. Where is she? *Oh God, I'm sorry for all the things I just told You. Please bring her back to us.*

"I'm going with you," Sarah was telling David in the other room. Her dress was wrinkled and her long hair was coming loose from its ribbon. She didn't care what she looked like. "Let's go now."

"All right," said David, tightening his arms around his wife. He'd returned and dismissed the good doctor just an hour earlier, but he knew he'd never sleep. The police had assured him that they were looking everywhere, but he had to do something.

He was reaching on the floor for Sarah's shoes when a knock sounded. "Come in," he said.

Easing open the bedroom door, Elsa stepped into the room. Her clothes were as wrinkled as Sarah's and her face looked as if she'd been beaten. She didn't venture any farther inside. Lifting her hands helplessly, she rasped, "I'm so. . .sorry."

It was hard for Sarah to look at her. If Elsa hadn't left the baby alone, Eileen would still be here. Sarah didn't trust herself to talk to the girl. All she wanted to do was scream, Why did you do it!

Just then, Elsa fell on her knees in front of Sarah and David. "I don't blame you for hatin' me, but you can't hate me near as much as I hate myself," she said between sobs. "If I could give my life to have her back, I'd do it."

Something broke inside Sarah. She reached out a trembling hand and put it on the girl's head. "I don't hate you, Elsa," she whispered.

Elsa lunged at Sarah's feet and threw her arms around her ankles. "I need you to hate me!" she cried. "I deserve it!"

"Now, Elsa," said David, his voice weak and unsteady. "You didn't mean for it to happen." He reached down to take her by the arm. "Please get up."

The girl heaved with sobs, but she finally let go of Sarah's legs and allowed David to help her to her feet. "I wish I could die," she cried between sobs.

Eileen stayed huddled in the corner of the new place, drawing her legs up to her chest whenever the big person came near. Her stomach hurt, and she looked around for her cup. Then she remembered it was back at the other place.

Another person, only a little bit bigger than herself, was standing by the big person with its hand held out. She saw the big person put something in its hand and turn away.

The not-so-big person came over to Eileen and squatted down. It had something in its hand that looked like the long rolls Willie Mae baked. The person put the thing in the dirt in front of her, tilted its head, and said, "swee tater?"

Eileen started to cry again. Mother was supposed to give her food, not these people. Turning her face to the rough stone wall, she wept until her throat became sore again. She fell asleep, huddled in the corner.

When she woke up, the people were gone, even the little baby. The thing was still on the dirt in front of her. Slowly, tentatively, Eileen touched it. It was soft where she mashed it with her finger, and something came out the color of the oranges Daddy sometimes brought home. Putting her finger up to her mouth, Eileen licked. The stuff was good and her stomach cried for more. She picked up the thing and bit into it. Making a face, she spit out the brown covering. She reached into the thing where she'd bitten and scooped out more of the soft insides.

When she'd eaten all that she could get out of the thing, Eileen looked around for her cup. The food had made her stomach feel better, but her throat was so dry that it was hard to think about Mother and Daddy. For the first time since she'd awakened that morning, she stepped out of her corner, keeping her eyes on the front door lest the big person come back in. A bucket was sitting on the bricks of the cold fireplace. She'd seen the others drink from it.

Climbing onto the bricks, Eileen crept up to the bucket. The handle to a metal dipper was leaning against the side. With both hands, Eileen tried to lift it to her mouth, but the water spilled in her lap and against the bricks as soon as she brought it out of the bucket. She tried again, and the same thing happened. Finally, she dropped the cumbersome dipper on the bricks and, propping herself with her arms, lowered her head into the bucket to drink. At first the water came up her nose and made her cough, but she was finally able to lap enough of it to satisfy her thirst.

Tugging at her soaked diaper, Eileen made it back to her corner and waited for Mother and Daddy to come for her.


Danny took slow, quiet steps past room twenty-one. He'd seen the doctor in the lobby, carrying his black bag and heading for the stairs. The baby hadn't been found, and Miss Abby had told him that the doctor probably had to give Elsa and the people she worked for something to help them sleep.

He'd looked for the baby all day as he worked, just in case she'd gotten lost here at the hotel. He had forced himself to check the dreaded cellar. When he'd almost changed his mind outside the cellar door, he imagined the baby down in that darkness with the spiders and rats.

Something was bothering him, nagging at his mind. When he'd mentioned to Miss Abby that he was still looking for the baby, she'd told him that the baby wasn't lost, but had been taken by someone bad. That had reminded him of something, but he could only remember a little bit of it. All he could picture was someone asking him about the baby, but he couldn't see the person's face. Perhaps it had been a dream. He had dreams all the time, and they always seemed real. Maybe he'd dreamed about someone asking him about the baby.

All day, Sarah had imagined the mistreatment her daughter could be suffering at her kidnapper's hands. She needed relief from her tortured thoughts so she accepted the laudanum from Doctor Thompson without protest. Once she'd taken the dose, she turned her face to the wall and waited for the numbness.

David had to order Elsa to take the laudanum. "I don't deserve to sleep," she'd protested. "Give me enough to make me die, and I'll take it."

David had gone into her room at the doctor's request. "Take the medicine, Elsa," he said. "You need your rest."

"I'm so sorry, Mr. David." She shook her head. "I have to think. . .have to remember what happened."

"You've gone through that with the police. Now I want you to sleep."

Violet knelt by her cot in the storeroom, her head in her hands. She'd gone to see Sarah at noon. Her friend had sat at a window and watched the street, barely acknowledging her presence. Elsa had been even worse, curled up in a ball on her bed.

"Please, Lord," Violet prayed. "You've been so good to me. I'd trade all my blessings if You could bring Eileen back to her family."

## eleven

At six o'clock Saturday morning, the doorman removed the bar that held the hotel front door secure. He was about to head for the courtyard entrance to do the same, when something white caught his eye.

Puzzled, he bent down and pulled out a sealed envelope that had been shoved under the door. When he saw the name on the envelope, he turned and ran up the stairs.

A policeman with bleary eyes answered the door to suite twenty-one. The doorman handed him the envelope. After turning it over in his hand and considering whether to break the seal, the policeman asked the doorman, "Can you send a message to Inspector McNeely right away?"

"The fact that the kidnapper has contacted us is a good sign," said police inspector Edwin McNeely, his beefy hands clasped behind his back as he paced the sitting room carpet. "At least we know that it wasn't someone who wanted a baby to keep."

"But what if he takes the money and doesn't bring back Eileen?" David shuddered. "I don't know how we can live much longer like this."

"That's why I think it'd be best to try to catch this. . .this devil when he tries to pick up the money. I hate to tell you this, but I think once he gets his hands on the money and can get away, he won't hang around in town long enough to get a message to you on the whereabouts of your baby.

Prison and all that."

"I just don't know. The letter warned not to involve the police."

"I know," said the inspector. "That's why we can't afford to make a mistake. Trust me, I'll have every man I can spare on this dressed in civilian clothes. We'll set a net so tight that nobody can get away."

He stopped pacing and looked at the letter again. "One thing though. I wonder why it says that the money has to be delivered by the dummy who works here. Do you know who. . .?"

The policeman assigned to stay with the Adams cut in. "Sir, if I might?"

"Yes?"

"There's a simple bloke named Danny employed here. Does odd jobs around the place and sleeps in the attic."

"Why would the kidnapper pick him?"

The policeman shrugged. "Maybe to keep you from sending one of us in disguise."

"Is there any way the boy could be involved in this?"

"I've talked with him a couple times in the hallway. He don't seem to have a mean bone in his body. Kinda pleasant fellow, if you ask me."

"Well, I'll have to talk with him," said the inspector. "And the people that work around him. He's not gonna be able to fool me if he's part of all this."

"Are you going to tell him about delivering the money?" asked the policeman.

"Not yet. We can't let any of this leak out."

Sighing, David rubbed his forehead. "If the kidnapper realizes that you know. . . ."

"You're too involved in this to think rationally," the

man cut in sympathetically. "We can't take the chance of this scoundrel disappearing into thin air." He came to a halt in front of a window. Squinting his eyes, he looked through the glass at the street below. "There are lots of places to disappear in England."

"Then I need to start raising the money."

Inspector McNeely raised his eyebrows. "Will that be a problem? Five hundred pounds is more than I could raise in a hundred years."

"I think I can persuade the bank that my company does business with to cash that large a check. My account in Charleston is good for it."

"Can you keep them from knowing what it's for? We can't let this ransom news get out, or the kidnapper'll realize we're involved."

"It won't be a problem."

"Good. Then I'll start the plans on my end." He lifted his hat from the table and brushed a piece of lint from the crown. "Your wife, sir. Are you going to tell her about this letter?"

"I tell her everything. She'd want to know."

"Do you mind if I make a suggestion?"

"Suggestion?"

"Your wife—Mrs. Adams. I spoke with Dr. McIntyre last night. He says she won't eat, and he has to give her more laudanum than he should to make her sleep. Quite frankly, he's worried she's on the brink of a nervous breakdown."

David closed his eyes and trembled.

"Sir?" The policeman assigned to the suite rushed forward. Taking David by the arm, he guided him to one of the chairs.

When David had regained his equilibrium, he looked up at the inspector. "What are you suggesting?"

"Get her out of the city. Send her somewhere where she can wait this out. Even a hospital."

"Sarah is stronger than she appears," insisted David. "She'd never forgive me if I sent her away."

"Perhaps you're right, but—"

"But what?"

"I've seen what tragedy, especially involving a child, can do to good, decent people. I'm not sure your wife can handle knowing that someone is asking a ransom for your baby."

Finally Eileen was able to crawl out of her sodden diaper, leaving it on the dirt floor. She started to cry for her Mother and Daddy again but remembered that the big person was in the room. The big person had made her arm hurt after Eileen had cried for a long time last night. She had cried even louder, but the big person had pinched her until she knew that she had to stop crying.

The big person was lying in the bed at the other end of the room, making loud noises with her mouth. Eileen got to her feet and walked over to the bucket to lap up some water. She heard whimpering and turned to look at the baby on the floor. It was lying on its back, waving its thin legs and arms in the air.

Getting down to her knees, Eileen crawled over to the baby and touched it on the cheek. The baby's hand latched on to Eileen's finger and put it in its mouth. Alarmed, Eileen tried to pull it back, but the baby's gums had a firm grip on the finger. It didn't hurt, so Eileen sat by the baby and let it suck on her finger.

Sarah got up from bed and wiped her eyes. The laudanum was still in her system, so she had to stand for a minute before trying to take a step. She caught her image in the framed mirror above the dresser. Her hair hung loose in tangled locks. *I look like an old woman,* she thought, reaching up to touch the dark circles under her eyes. She reached for her brush and then drew her hand back. *What does it matter what I look like?* Nothing mattered except having her baby back in her arms.

Sarah walked into the sitting room and saw David having breakfast with the policeman. She felt a stab of betrayal—how could David think of eating when Eileen was missing?

"Sarah," he said, coming to his feet. She immediately regretted her anger. His suffering was all too evident.

"Come have some breakfast," he suggested, his eyes full of concern. He pulled out a chair from the table. "Please?"

Sarah's stomach was a hard knot, but she knew that she should eat something, if only to make David happy. She sat down in the chair he held out for her and watched as he spread some marmalade on a soft roll and put it on her plate. He cut a couple slivers of yellow hoop cheese and laid them down next to the roll. "Would you like me to send for an egg or two?"

"No," she said. She stared at her food and made herself pick up a slice of cheese while David poured a cup of hot chocolate into her cup. "What about Elsa?" she asked after taking a sip of her chocolate. "Has she eaten anything?"

"I had a tray sent inside her room so she wouldn't have to face us. I don't think she'll eat."

Setting down her cup, Sarah asked, "Have I been that hard on her?"

David shook his head. "But I think she knows what we're thinking every time we look at her. She blames herself for everything."

"I know."

The policeman, finished with his plate, cleared his throat. "If I can be excused, ma'am, I'll stand out in the hall for a bit."

When he'd closed the door behind him, Sarah let out a sigh. "We need to talk to her. I don't blame her any more—it could have happened when the baby was with one of us."

David nodded. "You're right. I've blamed her, too. Before we talk to her, though, I want to ask you to do something for me. I want you and Elsa to go out to Julia Martin's and stay until we find Eileen."

"No."

"Sarah, you can't help her by staying here and grieving to death. Every time the door opens you look so hopeful, and then when its not good news, you look like you want to die."

"I want to die," she mumbled, looking down at her plate. "May God forgive me, but I do."

"Don't even think like that!" David swallowed hard before he was able to speak again. "Eileen will need you more than anyone else when she comes home."

"When she comes home?" she watched him warily. He'd averted his eyes from hers, but she'd caught something different in his expression. "You *know* something, don't you?"

"I just—"

Sarah leaned forward and sought his eyes with her own. "David, tell me." Her eyes widened and a groan escaped her lips. "She's dead, isn't she? You're trying to protect—"

"Sarah!" His voice was sharp in spite of the tears in his eyes. "Do you think I could sit here and talk over breakfast if our baby were dead? I love her, too, you know!"

Blinking, Sarah took his hand. "I'm sorry," she said, her voice unsteady. "I know you love her. But please, please tell me what you're keeping from me."

David sighed, closing his eyes. "We were sent a letter a little while ago. The person who took Eileen will give her back for five hundred pounds."

"Oh, David!" Sarah cried, covering her mouth with her hand. "Let's get the money right now!"

"The kidnapper wants it delivered in a canvas oat bag to a rum house called The Mermaid's Harp in three days."

"Three days!"

He nodded wearily. "It'll take us at least two to get the money. The kidnapper must know somehow—maybe from the newspapers—that we're from overseas. He 'thoughtfully' gave us time to raise the ransom." David's hands, resting on the table, curled into fists. "If I ever find the person who took our baby, I'll kill him. God forgive me, Sarah, but I'll kill him with my bare hands."

She believed him. David was the most gentle man she'd ever known, but he was extremely protective of his family. "David," she began, pushing aside her uneaten food. "I want to wait here with you."

"But the police will be coming in and out, more than before. They want to find the kidnapper before the three days are up. I don't think you can take the strain. Please think about. . . ."

Sarah's temples pounded, and she couldn't hear the rest of his sentence. "I'm staying!" Her chair fell to the floor behind her as she jumped to her feet. "She's out there somewhere, and I'm not leaving this city."

Not sure where she was going, Sarah went to the door and pulled it open. Barefoot and disheveled, she was down the hall and on the staircase in seconds, ignoring the sound of David's footsteps. "Sarah, please wait!" she heard as his hand grabbed her arm.

She jerked away and, with David at her heels, ran down the steps to the lobby, where the confused-looking doorman opened the door for them. Outside the hotel, she turned to her left, ignoring her husband's attempts to get her back inside.

The street was full of people. Sarah studied each face as it passed, wondering which one belonged to her daughter's kidnapper. Something caught her eye and she froze.

Eileen! In front of a bakery stood a navy blue pram, just like Eileen's. The fact that her baby's pram was under the hotel stairwell didn't shake her assurance that her baby was back.

Her heart pumping, Sarah ignored the staring people and ran toward the bakery with her arms outstretched.

"Sarah!" came David's voice again as he grabbed her arms from behind.

"Let me go!" she screamed. She could see a little hand moving in the air above the pram, Eileen's hand. With tears running down her face, Sarah almost flew the last few feet. Looking inside the pram, she gave a sharp cry. A bald-headed baby much younger than Eileen blinked at the sudden appearance of a stranger, then chuckled.

"No!"

Before David could stop her, she was throwing her weight against the plate glass door to the bakery. "Whose baby is out here?" she demanded.

All conversation died as the half-dozen people inside turned their faces toward her. A young woman standing in front of the counter gave her a puzzled look. "Ma'am?"

"Is that your baby? Did you leave your baby outside?"

The young woman paled, then started for the front door. "Has something happened. . .?"

"You'd better be glad that it hasn't!" Sarah shrieked to the woman as she passed.

The owner of the bakery was coming from behind the counter toward them. "Please get your wife out of here," he said to David, "or I'll have to send for the police."

"I'm sorry," David said, putting his arm around Sarah's shoulder. Silent, she did not pull away. "Our baby was taken just two days ago, and—"

"I know." The man's face was full of compassion. "I read it in the newspaper, and figured you were the people. Now, you'd best get your wife some help."

The young woman with the pram was just outside the door. "We're sorry," mumbled David as they passed.

When they got back to the hotel room, Sarah went to their bedroom and took her valise from the wardrobe.

"I'm ready to go to Julia's," she said flatly.


Violet was tying the strings to her bonnet when she heard the bell over the door to the shop.

"Violet?" came Jacob's voice from the other side of the storage room curtain.

"Come in."

Drawing aside the curtain, he stepped inside the storeroom. There was hardly room for him to walk, for they hadn't had time to shelve the new bolts of cloth that Mr.

Gilliatt had sent. "Your young lady friend is here to see you," he said. "I belieff I shall go upstairs for a minute."

Elsa stood in the shop with a carpetbag in her hand, looking more like a lost little girl than a young lady.

"I was just about to leave for the hotel," Violet said after embracing the girl. "Any news about Eileen?"

"Whoever took her wants a ransom, and Mr. David's tryin' to raise the money."

"Oh, mercy!"

"Nobody's supposed to know, he says, so we have to keep it quiet. Even the police ain't supposed to get involved. It's too late for that, though."

"How are Sarah and David taking it?"

"Bad. Mr. David wants me and Miss Sarah to stay with her friends out in the country."

Violet grimaced. "Sarah's getting worse?"

"Yes, ma'am."

"I want to see her before she leaves." She was about to retrieve her purse when Elsa said, "She's already gone."

Her eyebrows raised, Violet looked at the girl's gaunt face. "But you said David wanted you to go with her."

"I quit my job," said Elsa, wiping her nose with a handkerchief.

"You what?"

"I know it'll be easier for Miss Sarah if she don't have to look at me." Elsa spoke rapidly. "I have to stay in town, you see. I want to go back to all the shops that I passed that day and ask if anybody remembers seein' me and Eileen. This mornin' I realized that if I retrace my steps at the exact same time of day, maybe some of the same people will be on the streets."

"But haven't the police—"

"Don't you see? It might make *somebody* remember seein' me. I'll wear the same dress, the green calico."

"But where are you gonna stay?"

Elsa's eyes became pleading. "Can I stay with you 'til I find Eileen? I've got a little money saved, and I won't be no trouble. I can sleep on the floor."

*She's serious!* thought Violet.

"Please?"

In spite of her better judgment, Violet nodded. "First I want to tell David where you are. He's got enough to worry about. And only until Eileen is found." She held up her hand to ward off the girl's thanks. "I want you to give me your word about something."

"Anything," Elsa answered quickly, relief flooding her face.

"You have to ask David and Sarah for your job back when all this is over. They care about you, more than you know."

After a brief hesitation the girl said, "I will."

The trees grew more dense and the roads more narrow and uneven as the carriage left Bristol. Fields separated by hedges graced the surrounding hills, and an occasional rabbit lifted itself on hind legs to stare.

The driver pulled the horse to a stop in front of a majestic Gothic house, its brickwork veneered with white stucco and its crocketed pinnacles pointing to the sky. He hopped down from his seat and opened the carriage door.

"Shall I come back later?" he asked after David had helped Sarah to the ground.

"No. I need to get back to the city. Why don't we see if you can water your horse?"

Just then a tall ruddy-faced man appeared from the yard. "Would ye be Mr. and Mrs. Adams?" he asked in a relaxed Cockney accent while removing his cap.

Sarah's face showed the first sign of life since she'd left the city. "Leslie?"

The gardener bowed slightly. "I was wondering if you'd remember me, Miss Sarah. Me wife, Ginny's, been all a-twitter about seein' you again. She's upstairs feedin' the little one or she'd be out here to see ye."

David tensed at the mention of a baby in the house. *Perhaps this wasn't such a good idea after all.* He watched his wife's face for any sign of renewed hysteria.

Sarah's expression darkened, but she managed a smile. "And Frances and Agnes, are they here?" Along with Sarah, Ginny and Frances had been servants at Connelsworth Park when cruel Mrs. Gerty had been the owner. Agnes, kind and motherly, had been the cook.

"I'm afraid wee Frances married and moved off to Gloucester. But Agnes is still—"

His words were interrupted by a woman's voice. "Sarah!"

Coming down the carriage way toward them was an older woman, her hand waving in the air.

Sarah took a step forward. "Julia?"

"It's me all right, bless your dear heart!" When she reached Sarah, Julia Martin enveloped her in a hug. "Josh brought a newspaper home from town last night. I'm so sorry!"

Her lips trembling, Sarah managed to pat the former housekeeper on the back. "There, there now." Straightening her shoulders, she said, "I'd like you to meet David, my husband."

Julia extended her hand. "I'm pleased to meet you— Sarah wrote all about your kindness in her letter."

"And she spoke of your kindness more than once to me." Julia had persuaded the sixteen-year-old Sarah to ask for employment with the Carltons, the elderly couple who brought her to America.

Sarah had never forgotten the housekeeper's kindness. She had told Mr. Carlton how Mrs. Gerty, with the help of a dishonest solicitor, had stolen Connelsworth Park years earlier from Julia's supposedly indebted family. Mr. Carlton had written to Julia, advising her to have another solicitor investigate the sale of the property. After an investigation that ultimately involved the police, the estate had been returned to Julia.

Julia Martin had been grotesquely thin when Sarah had last seen her. The years since had been good to her, and she looked to have gained at least three stone.

Leslie's face had grown beet red, and he was kicking at the gravel in the lane. "So sorry, ma'am—me mentioning our little one upstairs."

"Please don't apologize," said Sarah. "I'm happy for you both. But I hope you can understand that I'd rather not see the baby just yet."

"Of course," soothed Julia. "I'm so glad you decided to come on ahead. Agnes and I will take good care of you." Turning to David, she asked, "Are you staying too, Mr. Adams?"

"Please call me David. I appreciate your invitation, but I'll be leaving for town as soon as we can get the horse taken care of." He turned to Leslie. "Do you mind showing. . .?"

"Right away, sir."

As Leslie ran for a bucket of water, David took Sarah's hands. "We're going to have our baby back soon," he whispered, his green eyes locked with her brown ones. "Please believe that."

Her lips were trembling, but she nodded. "I believe you."

Minutes later inside the swaying carriage, David covered his face and cried, "Oh Lord, help me to believe it, too!"

# twelve

"Elsa, wake up," ordered Violet, bending down to shake her shoulder.

Elsa stirred but did not open her eyes. She lay on a pallet Violet had made next to her cot.

"Wake up!"

Blinking, Elsa managed to focus her eyes on the brown face staring down at her. "Violet?"

"It's time to get up. You can roll your quilt and put it in that corner."

Elsa groaned. "Please let me sleep a little longer. I kept waking up last night and I feel awful."

"I know," Violet said sympathetically. "I heard you talking in your sleep. Nightmares?"

"I kept dreaming about Eileen. A black person was taking her away and she was crying."

"Black person? You mean a Negro?"

Elsa shook her head. "No. I couldn't see the face—everything was covered up. I tried to follow them, but my feet wouldn't move fast enough. What do you think it means?"

"I don't know. Maybe the Lord's tryin' to jar your memory about something."

"Well if He was so interested in helping her, why would He let her get taken in the first place?"

"Elsa!"

"He could'a struck the kidnapper down with lightening

or somethin'. You told me that God watches over His children. Where was He?"

"God hasn't forgotten that baby. He's with her right now." Bending down, Violet snatched Elsa's top sheet. "Now come on. I want you to get cleaned up. You're startin' to look awful."

"What does it matter what I look like?" Elsa murmured listlessly.

"It matters to me," snapped Violet. "I have to look at you."

When she noticed the stern expression on her friend's face, Elsa decided to keep quiet. She got up quickly.

"Why are you so dressed up?" she asked as she rolled her quilt and sheet into a bundle.

"I heard about a church for Negroes not too far from here. You need to hurry so we won't be late."

"But I need to look for Eileen."

"You can look when we get back. Won't do you any good today, anyway. The shops are closed, and the same people won't be on the streets."

Elsa stooped down to set her pillow at the end of Violet's cot. "But I'm not a Negro."

"You just noticin' that? I'm sure they'll be glad to have you worship, too. I'm worried about the way you been thinking about God. Now I've brought you a pitcher of warm water, so let's get going."

Elsa swallowed the protest that rose to her lips. After all, Violet had taken her in when she had no where to go. In an attempt to make amends, she said meekly, "Your hair grows fast."

Violet glanced in the mirror over her dresser and patted her curly dark hair, which was beginning to look feminine again. "Well, it's been near a month."

"Maybe there'll be a handsome man at church, just lookin' for a nice seamstress to marry."

"The things you say!"

Elsa looked on the verge of a grin as she said, "You never can tell."

Putting her hands on her hips, Violet said, "Well, if he shows up at church, I won't get to meet him because you're gonna run us late."

Elsa came to life, grabbing her towel from a nail on the wall. "I'll hurry!"

In the old cottage, dust particles floated in streaks of sunlight that managed to sneak through the grime-smeared window. Eileen reached out to touch her mother's cheek, but Mother was not there. She managed to sob quietly so the big person wouldn't get out of bed and yell at her.

Eileen hadn't been back to her corner since she'd seen a small thing with a long tail chew the hard part of her sweet potato. Anyway, it was warmer next to the baby at night—warmer than resting on the cold stones in the corner.

The not-so-big person drank some water from the bucket. When it saw that Eileen was awake, it refilled the dipper and smiled, motioning for her to come.

Eileen was thirsty, so she rolled over to her belly, rose to her knees, and stood up. She tottered over to the not-so-big person, leaned forward, and opened her mouth. Carefully, it held the dipper to Eileen's lips and let her drink.

"Want to go play?" asked the not-so-big person. It went to the door and pushed it open, then stood in the sunlight and motioned for Eileen to follow. Eileen walked over to the doorway, but stopped when she saw all the trees. What if the big dark person was out there? She turned around and went back to sit by the baby.

The big person was awake a few minutes later and made some angry noises with its mouth as it walked over to close the door. It looked at Eileen and made a face. "You stink."

The big person walked to a box and opened the lid. Presently it came toward Eileen with something that looked like Daddy's shirt. Eileen held her arms up obediently as the big person pulled her wet, soiled gown over her head, then stood there naked while the big person poured some water from the dipper onto a rag.

The wet rag felt cold, but when the dry shirt was pulled over Eileen's shivering body, it felt good. The big person rolled up the sleeves that dangled over Eileen's hands and turned away.


"Sarah, are you awake?" Standing in front of the bedroom door, Julia Martin shifted the tray she was carrying.

The door opened before she could knock. Sarah, dressed in a yellow striped poplin gown, stood in the doorway. She looked much better than she had the day before—the hair that had been so matted was washed and combed. Her skin, though, was pallid, and her eyes were shadowed with dark circles.

"Come on in, Julia," Sarah said as she reached for the tray. "You didn't have to do this—I was about to go downstairs."

"I didn't know if you were up to it," she answered, entering the room. "How did you sleep?"

Sarah closed her eyes for a second. "Not well. I should have brought some laudanum."

"I. . .I don't know what to say."

"Please don't be uncomfortable around me." Sarah sat down in a gold upholstered velvet chair by the window. "As much as I trust you, I'm not allowed to tell you everything that's happened lately. But I know I'll have my baby back soon."

Julia noticed that her friend's assuring words sounded forced and wondered if Sarah were trying to convince herself as well. She pulled out the bench from the dressing table and sat down. "How can I help you with the waiting?"

"Help me think about other things. Tell me what you've been doing since I left."

Crossing her knees, Judith smiled. The extra weight on her body softened the evidence of age, and her gray-streaked hair was loosely fashioned in a topknot. "Well, we've begun taking in boarders to help with the expenses of keeping up this place."

"I didn't realize that. How many?"

"Seven. No, eight, counting Miss Dwight--she came last week. It's good to have this house full of people. Makes for some interesting conversation around the table."

Sarah was reminded of times when meals were rushed so that the servants could get back to Mrs. Gerty's never-ending list of chores. "Is Mrs. Gerty still. . .?"

"In the insane asylum?" The older woman shook her head. "She passed away last fall."

Noticing that Sarah's expression was darkening, Julia changed the subject.

"By the way, I'm engaged."

Sarah had just picked up her marmalade spoon. She held

it poised in mid-air. "You're getting married?"

Julia nodded shyly. "This fall."

"To whom?"

"His name is Walter Aertker—he's the vicar here. I became good friends with his lovely wife, Elaine, when they moved here six years ago. When she died three years later, well, Mr. Aertker and I drifted into a friendship."

Sarah realized suddenly that there was a smile on her own lips. It felt so good, if only for a few seconds, to think about something else. "And when did this friendship turn to love?"

Blushing, Julia looked down at her fingers. "I don't know that you'd call it love—not the romantic kind the young girls pine for. But we enjoy each other's company. It's a comfortable friendship—like we've known each other all our lives. I'll settle for that."

"Friendship's important for a good marriage," said Sarah. "I know most poems are about the romantic side of love." She paused when she noticed the color in Julia's cheeks. "Am I embarrassing you?"

"No," she murmured. "Please go on."

"I was going to say that there's not enough attention given to the friendship part. How can you keep loving someone who's not a good friend? I hope you'll be very happy."

"Thank you. And I hope you'll still be in England for the wedding. That, is if—" Julia broke off her sentence, but Sarah knew she was thinking about Eileen. *If your baby is back in your arms. If life ever becomes like it was before, and you can do normal things like go to weddings.*

Sarah's chest became so heavy that it took effort just to draw a breath. She put her napkin in her tray. "I believe I'd like to lie down for a while longer."

Her face drawn with concern, Julia came over to pick up the tray. "Is there anything I can do for you?"

Sarah put a hand on her arm. "You already have. You made me forget for a little while."

When her friend had closed the door behind her, Sarah sat down on the four-poster mahogany bed. She slid her hand over the embroidered spread to a pillow and pulled it to her. Hugging the pillow, she buried her head in its coolness until the white muslin pillowcase was soaked with her tears.

> *As Jacob with travel was weary one day,*
> *At night on a stone for a pillow he lay:*
> *He saw in a vision a ladder so high,*
> *That its foot was on earth and its top in the sky. . . .*

There were no pews in Mr. Lowden's carriage house, just four long benches pieced together with lumber gleaned from the shipyard discard pile. One short bench against a wall was given over to two women, one quite elderly and the other cradling an infant. A dozen adults, counting Violet and Elsa, stood as they sang. Older children stood with their parents while the younger ones played quietly on the dirt floor behind the benches.

Violet noticed Deborah, the cook at Christopher's, and the woman smiled back at her. She wished she'd had time to speak with her before the service, but she and Elsa had made it just after the singing had started. Beside Deborah stood a tall, muscular man, his baritone voice resonant and clear.

She felt a jab at her side. Elsa had caught her watching

the man and was giving her a knowing look.

"I was just admiring his voice," Violet whispered through clenched teeth. "Besides, he's married."

The white-haired man in front of the small congregation led them in the next two stanzas of "As Jacob with Travel," a hymn she remembered singing back on the plantations. It felt good to sing with her people again.

Elsa was silent beside her. *I should've taught her some hymns while we were on the ship,* Violet thought. She hoped that the girl's bitterness toward God wouldn't last.

The next hymn was one Violet had learned in her church in Boston. As the group lifted their voices in harmony, she closed her eyes and made the hymn a prayer to her Savior.

> *My faith looks up to Thee,*
> *Thou Lamb of Calvary*
> *Savior divine!*
> *Now hear me while I pray,*
> *Take all my guilt away,*
> *O let me from this day*
> *Be wholly Thine.*

Elsa's lips trembled as the words to the song rang in her ears and sent conviction to her heart. She watched Violet's face, so radiant and trusting. *Why can't it be like that for me? Just as I was beginnin' to feel what it's like to have joy in my soul, it was snatched away.*

> *While life's dark maze I tread,*
> *And griefs around me spread,*
> *Be Thou my guide;*
> *Bid darkness turn to day,*

> Wipe sorrow's tears away
> Nor let me ever stray,
> From Thee aside.

Listening to the second stanza, Elsa wondered about the writer of the words. It seemed that he'd known the taste of tragedy and disappointment. *Nor let me ever stray. That's what I've been doing—straying. Blamin' God for everything.*

Still the question lingered: Why hadn't He prevented the kidnapping?

After the singing, all heads bowed for prayer. One of the men in the congregation thanked God for giving them a place to worship and asked for His continued blessings and mercy.

After the chorus of amens had finished, the man who'd led the singing opened the Bible and began to read with a stately British accent from the book of Ephesians: "For we wrestle not against flesh and blood, but against principalities, against powers, against the rulers of the darkness of this world. . . ."

Celly frowned at the noise which had awakened her so early. Reaching an arm over from her mattress to the floor, she grabbed the uncorked gin bottle and took a swallow. She wiped her mouth with the back of her hand and turned disgusted eyes toward the man who lay beside her. His mouth lolled open, showing blackened teeth under a beaked nose.

*When I'm rich, I won't look at trash like this,* Celly thought. Leaning on one elbow, she shook the man's shoulder. "Hey! Time to go."

His snoring stopped for a second, then became louder. "Hey! Wake up!"

With an abrupt snort, the man opened his eyes. He glanced around, trying to get his bearings. Finally his bloodshot eyes rested on Celly's face. "Hullo, lov," he mumbled, his fetid breath making her want to gag.

"It's time to go," she said flatly. "My husband'll be home any minute."

The man's mouth dropped open, sending more stench her way. "Your hus. . .?"

Celly gave the man's arm a shove. "Any minute. He killed the last bloke he found here."

When he'd left, Celly took another drink of gin and settled back down for more sleep. She closed her eyes and hummed. *Two more days.*

After the final amen had sounded, Deborah walked over to Violet and gave her a hug. "I was worried that you weren't going to come," she said.

"Wild horses couldn't have kept me away. I'd like you to meet my friend, Elsa."

Elsa smiled and took the hand Deborah offered. "We were admiring your husband's singing," she said, pretending not to notice Violet's tightened lips. "Weren't we, Violet?"

"Yes," Violet answered flatly.

"My husband had to work today," said Deborah. "He's not here." She glanced over to where she'd been sitting. "You're talking about Luke Preston—he's a neighbor of ours. Got a beautiful voice, hasn't he?

Elsa nodded. "I'll bet his wife is proud of him.

"He's not married," Deborah told her. "I think he's too

bashful to ask anybody."

She then introduced them to the other members of the congregation, including each of the children. When it came time for Luke's introduction, he gave Violet a shy smile and shook her hand. "I'm pleased to meet you."

Violet's eyebrows lifted at the sound of his accent. "Are you from the States?"

"South Carolina. And you?"

"The same," she answered, grateful that Elsa was content simply to listen. "How did you get to England?"

He seemed embarrassed to talk about himself. "I stowed away on a British ship we were loading. What about you?"

"I came over with some friends. They pretended I was their slave."

"Sound like good people."

"The best." Violet's eyes grew sad, and she felt Elsa stiffen. "Unfortunately, their baby was kidnapped a couple days ago."

The man's face was filled with concern. "I heard about that at the shipyards where I work. I been praying for that baby."

"Thank you. Please don't stop."

"I won't. Well, it was good to meet you," he said and stepped away. Seconds later he turned back. "Why don't we do that right now?"

"Pray? That would be wonderful," said Violet.

Asking her to wait, he went over to the pastor, who looked at Violet and Elsa and clapped his hands for attention. "Brothers and sisters!"

Conversations died down, and everyone watched him expectantly. "Brother Luke here tells me some bad news. You may have heard about the Americans whose baby was stolen."

While a few members of the congregation looked puzzled, most nodded or turned sympathetic glances towards Violet and Elsa.

"The child has not been returned. Those of you with children can understand the pain these people are going through. Before we leave for our homes, why don't we join hands and pray that our Father will protect the child and reunite her with her family. It was our Lord Jesus himself who said, 'Where two or three are gathered together in my name, there am I in the midst of them.'"

The pastor took the hand of the elderly woman next to him, who reached for Luke's hand. The rest of the small congregation followed his example until a circle was formed that stretched to the brick walls.

Expectant silence filled the room. Violet, unwilling to let go of the woman's hand on her right or Elsa's on her left, let tears run down her cheeks and drip off her chin. She heard Elsa sniffling and knew she was doing the same.

The pastor began to pray, his voice low and full of grief. He asked his heavenly Father to give the child's parents grace during this trial. "And please take care of the little one and bring her safely home."

Amens chorused around the room, and people began to leave.

"Will you come back next week?"

Violet looked up to see Luke standing nearby, his face anxious.

Still touched by the prayer, she could only nod.

As she and Elsa started walking back to the center of town, Violet turned and saw Luke walking in the opposite direction, alone.

They were halfway to the shop when Elsa touched her arm. "Violet?"

"Yes?"

"What that preacher said, about wrestling against princes?"

"Principalities," Violet gently corrected. "And powers."

"That's it. What did he mean?"

"Well, when someone does something to hurt us—"

"Like the kidnapper?"

Violet nodded. "It's not just the kidnapper we're fighting against."

"It's not?"

"I'm sure of it. The powers of darkness control people who are evil like that. We have to fight against those powers."

Elsa looked confused. "How can we fight something we can't see?"

"The same chapter of the Bible that the pastor read from says we have to put on the whole armor of God. Do you know what it says is the most important part of that armor?"

"What?"

"The shield of faith," Violet explained. "Remember the faith you had when you asked Jesus to save you?"

Elsa nodded.

"Have you had that same faith when you've prayed for Eileen? Or have you been blaming God?"

Elsa mumbled, "I've been blamin' God."

Violet's face was sympathetic. "It's natural to want to do that when things go wrong. But it don't mean anything if you have faith when life is good. You've got to have it through the bad times, too. In fact, the bad times strengthen our faith."

"You make it sound like we should want bad things to happen."

"Not at all, child," Violet was quick to answer. "I don't like misery any more than the next person. But when I've gone through them—bad times, I mean—holding on to my Savior's hand, they've made me stronger."

"Like when you were in jail?"

"For sure. When another bad time comes, I can look back and see how Jesus brought me through the last one. That gives me faith He'll see me through it again."

They had just reached the shop. Jacob opened the door, beaming. "I haff made some delicious soup," he exclaimed as he ushered them in. "You must come haff lunch with me."

"You are so kind," said Violet. "And I'm starving! We'll be upstairs in a minute."

"I don't like working on Sunday," said Violet a few minutes later as she untied her bonnet strings. "But I can't let Jacob organize all this cloth by himself."

Elsa looked uneasy as she studied the work to be done. "I can help, but can it wait 'til tonight? I want to see if there's anybody who saw me with Eileen, while it's still daylight."

"I understand. But please have lunch first. Jacob will be hurt if you don't."

"All right." Elsa hesitated. "Do you think God is mad at me? You know, for blamin' Him."

Violet smiled and shook her head. "He understands that you're learning."

"That's good. Because before I leave, I want to tell Him how sorry I am for thinkin' that way. Do you think that'll make my faith stronger?"

Violet reached out and squeezed Elsa's hand. "I'd say that's a good start."

Inspector McNeely smoothed out a piece of paper so David could see. "I looked over The Mermaid's Harp myself, and this is the layout. It's a big, crowded place, which works against us in one way and for us in another."

David nodded, studying the sketch with tired eyes. "It'll be easier for your men to blend in with the crowd."

"But it'll be harder to watch everybody," said McNeely. "Don't worry. We'll have our eyes on Danny every minute."

"Have you told him?"

"I've talked with the manager here, Mr. Harold. He's given permission for the boy to run this little errand Tuesday night. But he suggested not telling Danny the whole story until the very day."

"Why?" asked David.

"The longer he knows about it, the greater the chance of his accidentally mentioning it to somebody. We can't have people knowing that a retarded boy will be carrying that much money across town in a sack."

"You think he's not in with the kidnapper?"

Inspector McNeely smiled. "Absolutely not. I met the boy. He's an innocent if there ever was one. But I have a man tailing him.

David's worried frown deepened. "I hope I haven't made a mistake, involving the police when the letter said not to."

"The way I remember it, you didn't have a choice," said the inspector. He laid a beefy hand on David's shoulder. "Now don't worry, son. Most of us have little ones of our own. We're committed to getting that baby back to you."

# *thirteen*

By late afternoon, Elsa's shoulders were sagging. True to Violet's prediction, the few people in the streets were families out for a stroll. Most she'd questioned had heard about the disappearance of the baby and were sympathetic, but none could help her. She had abandoned her characteristic shyness because of her intense desire to find Eileen.

Elsa considered going back to the shop and helping Violet and Jacob. She could get up early the next morning and come back. Surely she'd find a witness to the kidnapping then.

"Hey Elsa!"

She looked to her right. Danny was lumbering toward her, his face wreathed in smiles.

"I thought you were gone," he said. "Are you comin' back?"

Elsa shook her head. "No, Danny, not yet. But it's good to see you. I didn't get a chance to say good-bye last night."

"I looked all over the hotel, but I couldn't find the baby."

"You did? Thank you for looking."

His face clouded. "It makes me so sad. That was a nice little baby."

"I know," said Elsa. "I wish I could find out who took her."

"Who took her?" Puzzled, he scratched his forehead.

"She didn't get lost?"

Elsa noticed a bearded man in work clothes loitering nearby, apparently interested in their conversation. "No, Danny," she said, lowering her voice. "Someone took her from the pram when I. . .when I left it in front of the toy store."

She waited for his condemnation, but he only looked sorrowful. "That was a bad thing—to take the baby away."

"I know. I'm tryin' to find out who did it." Tilting her head, she studied the red tiled roof of the Palmer House Inn, just visible down the street. "You know, Danny, I had a dream last night about a person dressed in black. He was taking Eileen away."

Danny nodded. "I dreamed about a black dog one time."

"I remember something about the day Eileen disappeared," continued Elsa. "Before I left the hotel, there was a lady all dressed in black—even her face was covered."

"How did she see?"

"She had a veil over her face." Elsa pointed beyond his shoulder to the fish net displayed above the door to the fish market. "You know, like that. She could see through the holes. Anyway, she was standin' at the end of the hall, and that's the only time I remember seein' her in the hotel."

"I seen her too," said Danny.

Elsa looked startled. "You did? Was she staying there?"

"I don't know. I only seen her on the service stairs, but she weren't supposed to be there."

"When, Danny?"

Running his hand through his dark brown hair, he looked down at his shoes. "One day."

"Was it Thursday?"

"I don't know," he answered, obviously embarrassed

that he couldn't remember. "But she weren't Miss Celly."

"Who?"

"My friend, Miss Celly. I thought it was her, but she didn't talk to me on the stairs. Miss Celly always talks to me." He gave a happy smile. "She's my friend."

Elsa's shoulders fell as the glimmer of a tangible clue disappeared. "So you don't know who the lady was?"

Danny shrugged. "I don't know." His brow wrinkled with concentration. "Was she the bad person who took the baby?"

"That was just a dream I told you about," said Elsa. "But it's strange that I didn't think about that lady until after I had the dream. Maybe Violet was right."

Danny's face showed no comprehension but he nodded politely. "Maybe Violet was right."

Glancing back at the hotel, Elsa said, "Do you think you could go with me to talk with the desk clerk and some of the other employees? Someone else had to have seen that lady."

"All right." He looked pleased that he could help her in some way.

As they walked side by side to the hotel, Elsa worried about running into David. She didn't want to see her former employers until she could bring them good news. *Oh Lord, please let something come of this.*

She glanced over her shoulder. The bearded man was following at a discreet distance. When he saw Elsa looking at him, he stopped in front of a tobacco shop and studied its window display.

Celly hated Sundays. The gin palaces and rum houses weren't open, and the town was too quiet. Streaks of purple and orange spun hazily across the darkening sky, and somewhere in the distance, a church bell pealed out the Doxology.

Hugging her arms against the unexpected breeze coming in from the bay, she walked toward her flat. Customers would be out later, when decent people were in their houses. *Two more days, and I'll be out of this town. I'll go to Paris and buy a fine coach and have a footman to drive me around. Gowns too, and fancy wigs.* People wouldn't look down their noses at her then. Money made all the difference, and soon she'd have all she deserved.

*Maybe I should have asked for more.* She hadn't wanted to ask for more than Sarah's husband could raise, but what if they had much more?

Celly ignored the inebriated man weaving ahead of her on the sidewalk, usually an easy target that early in the evening. *I could send another letter—tell them I've changed my mind and need a thousand pounds. But then I'd have to give him more time. The longer I wait, the bigger chance somethin' can go wrong—it's too late to change things.*

*Oh well, it don't matter,* she thought. *The best part of all was that Little Miss Sarah Bluestocking wouldn't get her baby back anyway.* Celly grinned. Her mother was probably attached to the brat by now, and would gladly keep raising her with the others for a few extra shillings once in a while. Or she could send her to a charity home, for all Celly cared. She'd be in France with more important things to think about.


"Thank you, anyway," Elsa said as she left Danny in the lobby of the Palmer House Inn. Only one of the cook's assistants had seen the mysterious woman that Thursday afternoon, and she had been too busy preparing evening meals to think anything about it. When Elsa pressed her for details, the girl remembered a bit of red hair in back where the veil did not quite meet, but nothing else.

Danny was disappointed. He couldn't understand why the lady was so important, but it obviously mattered to his new friend. "I hope you find the little baby."

"Me too," said Elsa. "Or at least some clues I can give the police. Tomorrow I'm goin' to go back to that part of town and ask if anybody remembers seein' somebody dressed in black. Can't hurt."

"All right."

Before she turned to leave, Elsa put a hand on Danny's arm. "Somehow, I think this is important. While I'm gone, please try to remember anything you can think of about that lady."

"The lady on the stairs," he said, nodding. "I'll try real hard. Then will you come see me?"

"Tomorrow."


"I never thought I'd see this kitchen again when I left here," said Sarah. She, Agnes, Ginny, and Julia Martin were seated at the oak work table over mugs of hot chocolate.

"And how you've grown!" observed Agnes, the cook. She and Ginny had been cautioned to choose their words carefully around Sarah. They walked on eggshells to keep from mentioning anything to do with babies.

Ginny looked down at her own waist, which had thickened considerably over the past few years. "She hasn't grown as much as I have. It's the sweets. I can't let them alone."

"Eileen has a real sweet tooth," Sarah mused. "One of her first words was *cookie*." Catching Ginny's faint gasp, she looked up. "I'm sorry. I've been trying to think about other things all day, but everything reminds me of my baby."

"We understand," said Julia, putting a hand over Sarah's. "Would you like to tell us more about her?"

A tear came to the corner of Sarah's eye and hung there, glistening in the candlelight. "I don't know. It hurts to think about her, and it hurts not to think about her."

"We're so sorry it happened," said Agnes, her own eyes wet. "So sorry."

Sarah gave a weak smile. The tear had started a course down her cheek. "Not knowing where she is—that's the worst part of all this. I don't know where she is, who's with her, or anything. You're all trying to comfort me, and I appreciate it, but is anybody trying to comfort Eileen? When I think of how confused and sad she must be right now, I almost go crazy!"

"A fine poplin this is," said Jacob, unfolding a length for Violet's inspection. "There are six more bolts just like it."

Violet pointed to a place on one of the shelves in the store room. "Getting all this cloth is a real blessing."

Nodding, Jacob said, "Your friends vere kind to arrange this. Now ve can afford to hire an extra full-time seamstress or two, so you won't haff to vork so hard."

"That's a good idea. Not that I mind hard work, but I have a feeling we're gonna be real busy soon."

"Perhaps you should teach me to use a needle and thread as well," suggested Jacob with a twinkle in his eye.

Violet laughed. "You'll have enough to do, running this

place when we open again."

With a chuckle he reached down for another bolt of the poplin. Setting it in place, he paused again. "You know, I haff not laughed in such a long time. Thank you for reminding me how."

With a smile, Violet said, "I believe we're gonna be good business partners."

"It is funny," mused Jacob. "You are a Negro and a Christian, and yet I'm beginning to think of you as a daughter." Quickly he looked over his glasses at her. "Haff I offended you by saying that?"

"Not at all. Why would that offend me?"

The expression on his lined face was unreadable. "Because I am a Jew," he answered softly.

Violet put a hand on his arm. "That doesn't matter, Jacob."

"Then you do not blame me for killing Christ?"

"For killing Christ? Of course not!"

Taking off his glasses, Jacob wiped his eyes with the back of his hand. "I am sorry. For so long my family was called 'Christ-killers' in Poland, until finally ve vere run from our land. Later, some of the men in the shipyard here refused to talk to me. Now I can't help but vonder if every Christian I meet is thinking the same thing."

Sighing, Violet shook her head. "I didn't know that. It's so sad, what men do to each other sometimes. But every Christian doesn't think that way about Jews. The very Jesus we worship chose to be a Jew while on earth."

"Then vhy do some Christians hate us so?"

"Just because someone isn't a Jew doesn't mean he's a Christian," she answered. "Jesus loved the Jews so much, He said that He wished He could tuck Jerusalem under His wing like a hen with her chicks."

"I haff not heard such a thing," said Jacob.

"It's true. There's so much about Jesus that you—"

"My young friend," Jacob cut in with a gentle shake of his head. "Ve vill not speak of this right now."

"You mean you don't want me to talk about Jesus around you?" Violet asked. "How can I keep from talking about Jesus? He's the most important part of my life!

"I mean you and I will speak of this another time. I am old, and I haff believed a certain way all my life. Give an old man time to absorb these things you say."

Violet nodded. "I understand."

"Thank you." He gave her an affectionate smile. "It may be that I vill not embrace these beliefs you have, but I vill listen."

"Please try to remember," Elsa said Monday afternoon to the man sitting on the cobbler's bench, a half-finished boot in front of him. Dressed in the blue calico she'd had on the day Eileen disappeared, she'd questioned merchants and customers in every store within a block of the toy shop without success. The cobbler, however, had been too busy to speak with her until now. "I was right across the street in the toy store, and the pram was outside."

The man wiped his worn hands on his canvas apron and shook his head. "I already told the police that I didn't see any pram. I was busy with customers, you see."

"What about a woman in a black dress? Her face was covered with a veil. Did you see someone like that?"

He scratched his beard. "All in black, you say?"

Elsa's pulse quickened. "Did you see her?"

"Well, now, I believe I looked up and saw such a woman

in my window. Just for a minute."

"Did she have a veil over her face?"

"Don't rightly know. Her back was to me."

Turning to look through the man's front window, Elsa had a perfect view of the toy shop.


Eileen froze at the sound of footsteps just outside the door. The big person and the not-so-big person and the baby were inside. That meant someone else was about to come in. Was it her mother and father?

She heard knocking. What if it was the dark person? Eileen scurried to her old corner before the big person reached the door to open it.

A big person she'd never seen came into the room, carrying a sack on its back. It had bristly hair all over its face and little eyes that moved all over. The little eyes stopped moving when they came to Eileen.

"Do ye want to buy some rabbits?" the new big person was saying to the old big person.

"Already cleaned?"

The new big person shook its head. "But I kin skin one for you right now."

"Gimme one, then. All I can afford."

"That a new little girl?" the new big person asked.

"An orphan. Friend of my Celly's."

The smile that the new big person gave Eileen confused her. It wasn't the kind she was used to seeing on Mother's or Father's face. It made her press closer into the rocks of her corner.

Finally the new big person turned to the old big person. "Got half-a-dozen rabbits here. Trade 'em all to ye for the girl."

The old big person turned to look at Eileen.

"I'll skin 'em all for ye, too."

"I best not," the old big person finally said. "Celly might git mad."

The new big person looked at Eileen again. It licked its lips and turned back to the old big person. "Throw in a half-bottle o' good black stout."

The old big person was quiet. It took a step toward Eileen and turned back around. "Can't make Celly mad. She's gonna bring me some money."

"Well all right then. I'll skin your rabbit outside."

The courier from the bank, flanked by two uniformed policemen, carried the iron strongbox to suite twenty-one at the Palmer House Inn. After setting the box on the brick hearth, the man bent down, unfastened the lock, and swung the lid open.

"Five hundred pounds sterling," he said to David. "Do you want to count it, Mr. Adams?"

David shook his head. The pound notes in front of him represented a major part of his savings, but they meant nothing to him. Eileen was all that mattered. "Just lock it back up, please."

The courier fastened the lid back in place and left.

"Tomorrow's the day," Inspector McNeely said to David. "Are you getting nervous?"

"Very nervous. This is torture."

McNeely looked at the dark shadows under his eyes. "I'm sorry."

"Have you spoken with the boy yet?" asked David.

"Danny? Just a little while ago."

"Will he deliver the money?"

"Oh yes. I haven't told him the details yet, but he's agreed to run an errand for us tomorrow evening. I'm afraid to let him know everything—there'd be other people besides the kidnappers interested in a lad carrying that much money around."

A line creased David's forehead. "Sarah told me the boy was kind. I'd like to give him a reward when all this is over. After all, he's taking some risk."

"We're going to try to minimize that risk," assured the inspector. "I'll have men in the bar, and some strewn along the route he'll take."

"Are you sure they won't look like policemen? I don't want anything to go wrong."

"Don't you be worrying about that. These blokes will blend into their surroundings like chameleons."

"He's out back tidying up the courtyard," one of the maids said when asked about Danny's whereabouts.

Thanking her, Elsa walked down the main hall of the hotel and through the french doors leading to the courtyard and fountain. She spotted Danny under the shade of two giant oak trees, sweeping the flat stones of the walkway with a broom.

"Hello, Danny!"

The boy looked up and grinned. "Hello, Elsa! I was hoping you'd come to see me."

"Well, here I am." She glanced at the man seated on one of the lawn chairs nearby, reading a newspaper. "Do you have time to talk?"

"Just for a little while," he answered regretfully. "I don't want Mr. Harold to think I'm not doin' my job. He says I'm a hard worker."

"Then we'll talk while you work. Is that all right?"

Danny smiled. "That's a good idea—talk while I work. I can do both things at the same time."

Elsa watched for a few minutes as he began to move his broom again. "I found a man who saw the woman we're lookin' for."

"You did? With the black thing over her face?"

"The veil. The man saw her looking at the toy store from across the street. I don't know if it was while I was inside, but it seems strange that she was here at the hotel that same day."

Elsa noticed that the man with the newspaper was taking an interest in their conversation. *Could he be in with the kidnappers?* she wondered. *If so, why would he hang around Danny?*

Deciding the man was only a curious eavesdropper, Elsa went on. "I was wonderin' if you remembered anything else."

"About the lady in the black dress?"

"Yes."

Danny bent down to pull some weeds that had forced their way up between two rocks. "All I can remember is that I seen some red hair. And I thought it was my friend Miss Celly."

Elsa frowned. He'd mentioned that name before. "Does she live here in Bristol? Miss Celly, I mean."

"She lives by the water," he answered, turning to smile at her. "She's my brother's friend, too."

"Does she have red hair like the lady in the black clothes?"

"Red hair. But the lady didn't talk to me, and Miss Celly always talks to me."

Folding her arms, Elsa thought. "Maybe she didn't want you to know it was her."

"But why would Miss Celly do that?"

"I don't know, Danny. But think, does she know about the service stairs?"

Looking up from his broom, Danny was just about to shake his head when he remembered bits of a conversation with Celly a couple days before the baby was stolen. When she came to get some money for Raymond's medicine, she had asked him about the service stairs.

Danny closed his eyes and tried to remember why. A gust of wind lifted the shock of brown hair from his forehead and scattered the sweepings beside his broom.

"Oh no!" he cried, looking down at the leaves and bits of grass that had escaped their neat pile.

"It's all right," soothed Elsa, taking the broom from his hands. "Let me help you finish."

When the trash was finally back in a pile, she helped him sweep it into the burlap sack he'd brought along. "Now," she said, wiping her hands on her skirt. "Do you remember if your Miss Celly knew about the service stairs?"

Danny closed his eyes again. Someone had asked about the room number where the people with the baby lived. Had that been Miss Celly? But why would she ask him that?

Opening his eyes, he studied Elsa's face. She had been so nice to him, maybe even nicer than Miss Celly. He wanted to help her, but he didn't understand why she wanted to know so much about Miss Celly. He was sure Miss Celly wasn't the bad person who took the baby away.

He had to think some more, later, when he could lie in his cot and look up at the stars. Then he would remember who asked him about the room number to the suite, and why Miss Celly wanted to know about the back stairs.

"Can you come talk to me tomorrow?" he finally asked, feeling bad about disappointing Elsa.

Elsa sighed. "We haven't got much time. Do you think you'll have something to tell me then?"

"Tomorrow." She was about to leave when he thought of something. "Elsa?"

"Yes?" Her face was hopeful.

"Come in the morning—I have to do somethin' important tomorrow night."

## *fourteen*

That night after a supper, Danny carried a candle up the service stairs to the top landing. There were four tiny bedrooms in the attic, and his was to the left. He pushed open the door, and started at the sight of Celly seated on his cot.

"Hello, Danny-boy," she said. From the glow of the lamp stand he could see her black dress, and the black hat and veil sitting on the bed beside her. "How 'bout closin' the door?"

"You *was* the lady on the stairs!" he exclaimed, not moving.

"Me?" Celly looked puzzled. "Oh, that! I came to tell you something that day, but I got scared that Harold bloke would see me."

"But why didn't you talk to me?"

"Like I said, I was scared." She stood and smoothed the wrinkles from her dress. "I've brought you a present."

"A present?"

Walking over to where he stood, Celly blew out the candle in his hand and pushed the door shut. She smiled at him. "Look on your dresser."

Turning, Danny's eyes opened wide with wonder. On top of his battered oak bureau was a clear glass bowl of water. Two goldfish swam back and forth inside, their tails moving gracefully from side to side. "For me?" he asked as he stepped toward them.

163

"Just for you," she answered, taking a seat on the narrow bed again.

Filled with awe, Danny reached out a finger to touch the side of the bowl. "Thank you, Miss Celly. What are their names?"

"Well, they ain't got names. You'll have to think of some."

Getting down on his knees for a closer look, he studied his new pets. "I know!" he finally said. "I'll name them Celly and Elsa!"

"Fine with me," she said with a yawn. "Who's Elsa?"

"My new friend. She's nice, like you."

"That's good." Gathering up the hat and veil in her lap, Celly patted the side of the cot. "Come sit with me, Danny-boy. I want to tell you something."

Reluctantly he tore his eyes away from the goldfish and walked over to her.

"I've got this terrible problem," Celly began, her eyes downcast. "Just terrible."

Danny's eyes widened. "Are you cryin', Miss Celly?"

"Yes," she sniffed.

"Why? Did Raymond hit you again?"

"No," she said with a snort. "He's moved in with some other doxy. I'm sad 'cause I'm scared that little baby who got kidnapped is gonna get hurt."

"Really, Miss Celly?"

Celly sniffed again, then nodded. "Danny, did Mr. Adams ask you to deliver anything to The Mermaid's Harp tomorrow night?"

He shook his head. "A nice man that was with him asked me if I knew where it is, but he didn't tell me to take no money there."

*So they went to the police after all!* She wasn't surprised, but it wouldn't do them any good. "What did you tell him?"

"I told him I been there lots of times. Remember? You and Raymond used to take me there to sing."

Celly winced. "Did you tell him about me?"

"No, ma'am."

Patting his hand, she said, "Good. Now, let's talk about tomorrow night. The police are gonna ask you to take a sack of money there. It's for the person who took the baby."

He thought this over. "And if I give that person the money, will he bring back the baby?"

"Yes, that's what's supposed to happen."

A smile lit up his face. "Then Elsa won't have to look any more!" He wondered why Celly looked worried. "Miss Celly?"

"I was at Nooley's Pub just a little while ago and I heard some men talkin' about the kidnapper." Clucking her tongue, she added, "He's a terrible bad man—he might kill the baby if he don't get what he wants!"

Alarmed, Danny started to get up from the cot. "We have to tell the baby's daddy so he can get more money!"

"Wait, it ain't that simple," said Celly, putting a strong arm across his chest to keep him in place. "If you tell him about it, he'll be real sad, 'cause that's all he's got."

"Can't he get more?"

"Where?" She sighed. "He ain't got a good job, like you. I'm so worried that they're gonna lose that baby!"

Clasping his hands together tightly, Danny tried to think. He'd have a handful of bob when he got paid Saturday, but that would be too late.

"I know!" Celly's voice interrupted Danny's thoughts. "What if I added some more money to the sack—enough to make this kidnapper bloke happy?"

The boy's mouth fell open. "Could you do that?"

"It'd take me a bit o' time to raise it, but I'll bet I could have another hundred quid or so by tomorrow night."

"A hundred quid!" He couldn't picture that much in his mind. "Would that be enough to make him give back the baby?"

"I'm sure it would! The only thing is, I might not make it back here to give it to you before you leave."

"Could you come to The Mermaid's Harp when I get there?"

Pursing her lips, Celly turned to the window behind them and studied the rooftops below. "What if I meet you on the sidewalk just before you turn the corner to East Dock Road? I could take the bag for a second, put the extra hundred pounds in it, and give it right back. Then you can go in the saloon and do your good deed."

Danny stole a glance at the bowl on his dresser and wished he could go look at his new fish again. As much as he liked Miss Celly, all this planning was beginning to make him tired. "All right," he said, feeling guilty for hoping she would leave.

She put a finger up to his lips. "One thing, Danny. We can't mention this to nobody!"

"Not even the police?"

"Especially the police! I don't want nobody to know about my part in all this. I'll explain why when the baby's back safe with its mother and daddy."

"What if they see you give me the money?"

Celly gave a coy grin. "Trust me, people are used to

seein' me...take walks down that road. And they won't be surprised if I go up and talk to you for a minute or two." *Just long enough to switch bags—then it's off to the quay where me hired skiff awaits!*

Eileen lifted her head when the room turned suddenly dark. She could hear the big person moving the covers on her bed and knew it was time to go to sleep. The baby whimpered beside her. The urge to cry was so strong that Eileen could barely keep it in. She had to, though, for when she'd cried for her mother and father a little while ago, the big person had said, "I'm tired of your yelling!" and had put her outside.

That had been the most terrifying thing yet, for she imagined that the new big person with the rabbits was behind one of the trees, looking at her like he wanted to put her in his sack. She'd screamed at the door for so long, that the old big person had let her back in, telling her if she cried again she'd spend the night outside.

The dirt floor grew cold as the night grew darker. Eileen shivered under her rag that the not-so-big person had given her for a cover and snuggled closer to the baby. The baby was still whimpering, but it didn't move. Its arms were warm, much warmer than Mother's cheeks. The thought of Mother put an ache in her throat, but Eileen put her fingers in her mouth and was quiet.

After he'd watched the fish for a while, Danny realized he'd forgotten to think about the lady in the black clothes for Elsa. Telling his fish goodnight, he changed into his nightshirt, blew out his lantern, and climbed into bed.

Dozens of stars were sprinkled across the cloudless sky.

Folding his arms behind his head, Danny looked out the window at them.

*I knew that was Miss Celly on the service stairs! And Elsa said it was the same day that the baby disappeared.*

Suddenly Danny remembered Miss Celly asking him what room the family with the baby was staying in. *Why did she want to know about them?*

Another picture came to his mind—of a time when he'd just gotten this job. Miss Celly had come to borrow money, and Mr. Harold had told her not to come back to the hotel. "She's taking advantage of you, Danny," he'd said. "Besides, we don't want her kind around here!"

He hadn't known what Mr. Harold meant by *her kind,* but he'd needed the job. Raymond had moved in with Miss Celly, and Danny'd had no place to go.

Squinting his eyes, he made the stars blurry. Elsa had made the boys that were picking on him go away, and now she was looking for the baby. She never begged him to drink stuff that he didn't want to drink, and she never asked for money or got mad and called him Dummy.

He thought of his fish swimming quietly in the dark. "Miss Celly gave them to me," he said out loud. "She's my friend too."

But why had she given him a gift? She'd never given him anything before. *Somethin's not right,* he thought. But what was it? He wished he could talk to Elsa again. *Tomorrow morning,* he remembered. *She said she'd come back to see me.*

The hinges let out a shrill whine as Celly pulled open the door to her one-room flat. Across the room she caught a glimpse of herself in the spotted mirror hanging on the wall. *I've put on these horrible widow-clothes for the last time. After tomorrow it'll only be silks for me!*

"Hello, Celly."

She wheeled around, heart leaping in her throat. A man stood in the corner with his arms folded across his chest.

"Uh. . .Raymond!" she stammered. She held out her arms and stretched her lips into a smile. "I been so worried about you!"

Raymond's eyes, the color of lead shot, narrowed. "That's why you didn't come back with Danny's money last week, 'cuz you was so worried."

The color drained from Celly's face as she dropped her arms. "Danny didn't have enough money," she lied. "I tried to get some more, but I got beat up and robbed."

"Then why didn't you come back and tell me?"

"'Cause they left me for dead in a alley!" Her words tumbled out faster now. "When I came to, it was mornin' and you was gone!"

The corners of his thin lips curled. "You must be slippin', Celly, to make up a story like that."

"But it's true. I swear it!"

"Then how come you ain't got no scars, huh?" he asked menacingly. "'Cept those pits all over your face!"

Celly stepped back. "They hit me in the head!" She put a finger up to the crown of her head. "Right here, they did. There was a big knot there till yesterday!"

"Is that so?" Raymond had been edging sideways with cat-like steps. He was standing in front of the closed door. "Then how come you didn't ask none of my friends about me? Shorty knew where I was. He coulda told you if you'd asked him." He smiled again and reached behind his back, bringing out a long, steel-bladed knife from the waist of his trousers.

Taking another step back, Celly put a hand to her throat. "Raymond, listen!" she pleaded. "I was gonna look for you when I got some money!"

"Yeah?" He laughed, turning the knife blade over and over in his hands. "And when was that gonna be?"

"Soon! Then I was gonna find you and leave town with you!"

He stepped toward her and ran a stained finger along the edge of the knife. A drop of blood spouted on the tip of his finger.

Celly fought the urge to scream. It would enrage him further, and it wouldn't bring help. People in her part of town minded their own business. "More money than you ever saw, Raymond! For both of us!"

"Yeah?" Lifting an eyebrow, he said, "What'd you do, Celly, roll another drunk? You got a couple o'quid this time?"

Her back was against the wall, and Raymond was edging closer. "Five hundred pounds!" she cried desperately. "I swear it'll be ours soon!"

He shook his head. He could stretch out his arm and touch her with the tip of the knife if he wanted to. "Danny's gonna be so sad when he finds out you're dead."

"I stole a baby last Thursday!" she cried desperately. "Me mum's keepin' it for me."

"Ain't you got enough brats runnin' around that shack?"

In spite of her terror, Celly's face darkened. "One of em's yours! You never gave her a penny to raise it, either."

"Mine?" He spat on the floor. "There ain't no way to be sure o' that, is there?"

"These people are rich, Raymond, from the States!

Ain't you heard about the kidnapping?"

He paused inches away from her, and cocked his head to the side. "I ain't heard nothin'."

Celly lifted a fold of her black dress. "I was wearin' this dress with a veil over my face. I followed the baby's nanny and took it when she weren't looking."

Narrowing his eyes, Raymond studied her face. "So how are you s'pose to get the five hundred quid?"

She let out a quick breath. "I sent 'em a letter. They're gonna put the money in a barley sack and give it to Danny tomorrow night."

"To Danny!"

Keeping her eyes on the knife, she said, "Don't you see? He's the perfect one. Only I didn't mention him by name, see? I just said to have the dummy that works there deliver the money."

Raymond lowered his knife a little. Breathing easier, Celly continued. "That way, they'd think it was someone who's seen Danny around the hotel, and not somebody who knows him real good."

"And how's he s'pose to deliver this money?"

"He's to go inside and sit at a back table with the sack until someone comes up and asks for it. I said in the letter that I'd have people watchin' him different times the whole way there, and if there's any police or anybody who looks too interested, the deal's off."

Raymond shook his head. "The police can hide as good as anybody else. What's to stop the Americans from goin' to them anyway?"

"They already did, according to Danny. But that don't matter because I'll get the money *before* Danny gets to the saloon. And share it with you, of course," she hastened to add.

The man chewed his thin bottom lip. "How you gonna get your hands on the money?"

Celly pointed to a flattened barley sack lying on the floor by her mattress. "That's the kind of sack Danny's gonna have. And he's got to go down East Dock Road, where I do most o' my business. The street lamp is broken at the corner of Commerce Street—I made sure of that last night. I'll go up to Danny-boy with that sack under me cloak, only it'll be full o' rags."

"And then?"

"He's gonna hand me the sack he's carryin', thinking I'm gonna put more money in it. I'll just swap sacks with him." At ease now, she laughed. "The dummy'll be sitting in that saloon for hours, waitin' for someone to come up and ask for the money! By the time the police realize nobody's comin' and check the sack, I'll be. . .I mean, we'll be on the way to France!"

Raymond curled his lip in a mocking sneer. "France! How you gonna manage that?"

"I gave Whitey Perkins twenty-bob and promised him an extra twenty quid if he'd have his fishing boat waitin' tomorrow night."

"Where?"

"Just a bit down from the saloon, in front of the tobacco warehouse. He said he'll take me. . .us all the way to the coast of France."

Raymond snorted derisively. "Perkins' boat is a mite old. How do you know it'll make it that far?"

"He said it would," Celly assured him. "Says he's done it before."

"And all we have to worry 'bout is how to spend the

money."

Celly laughed. "We can go to Paris! Wouldn't we look like gentle-folk, ridin' around in a fancy carriage!"

Grinning, Raymond said, "Wouldn't that be somethin'!" He was still smiling as he raised the tip of the knife and thrust it through the bodice of her black dress and into her chest.

"The only thing is, Celly love," he whispered as she pulled at the knife handle, the surprise in her face giving way to terror, "it wouldn't look strange for Danny's brother to go up and chat with 'em too, and I can swap bags as good as you."

## fifteen

Elsa woke up early Tuesday morning after a restless night. *Tonight Mr. David has to pay the ransom,* she thought. *If only Danny's got something to tell me.*

Whether he did or didn't, she was going to the police. Surely they'd be interested in the veiled woman who'd been following her and Eileen that terrible day.

*Lord, I'm so worried that whoever's got Eileen will hurt her. Please watch over her and bring her back to us.* She was about to roll up her bed when she closed her eyes again. *And please help me to have more faith.*

In semi-darkness she dressed, moving around quietly so as not to disturb Violet. She knew her friend had stayed up late, pouring over dress patterns under the light of a single candle. *When all this is over, I'll buy a dress from her and Mr. Jacob—maybe I'll be their first new customer!*

Remembering what was to happen that night, Elsa's thoughts turned somber. *I love you Eileen, wherever you are.*

The doorman was unlocking the front door when Elsa arrived at the Palmer House Inn. "Danny should be coming down to breakfast about now," he told her with a smile. On her way to the kitchen, Elsa met Danny coming from the service stairway.

"Do you have time to talk with me before breakfast?" she asked. Even though he seemed glad to see her, there were shadows under his eyes and his shoulders were more

174

stooped than usual.

"I'm not hungry," he answered. "And I got to tell you something important. Do you want to sit in the lobby?"

"Will you get in trouble?"

"I don't have work to do 'til breakfast is done. Then I help in the kitchen."

The two walked to the lobby and sat on a plush velvet sofa. "Why ain't you hungry?" she asked. Out of the corner of her eye, she saw the man who had been in the courtyard sit in an armchair behind them. Straightening his newspaper, he began to read.

"I feel too bad to eat," Danny said, unaware of the man's presence.

"Why?"

"I think Miss Celly don't really like me,"

Elsa's heart sank. Surely Danny had something, anything to tell her that would lead to the woman in black.

"And maybe she took that baby."

"What?" Elsa closer to Danny and lowered her voice. "You think your friend's the kidnapper?"

Danny nodded. "I was lookin' at the stars last night, and I had to think a long time, but I figured it out." The corners of his mouth trembled and he began to blink away tears. "Miss Celly ain't my friend at all. Even Raymond don't really like me."

Elsa put a hand on the boy's shoulder. "Well, I like you, Danny. You're one of the nicest people I ever met."

"Really?"

Elsa smiled. "Really." As much as she would have liked to cheer him up, she didn't know how much time they had left. "Now Danny, please tell me why you think Miss Celly's the kidnapper."

"Miss Celly asked me about the soot that the people with the baby are stayin' in. She asked me about the stairs, too."

"You said you thought it was her in the black clothes. Was it?"

"It was her."

Elsa's pulse raced. She wanted to jump up and go to the police, but she had to be sure. "Do you remember anything else?"

He spoke slowly, as if he had to concentrate on the right words. "Miss Celly gave me a present last night and was nice to me. Then she told me that I'm goin' to bring the money from the baby's daddy to the kidnapper tonight."

"You are?" Her eyes widening, Elsa said, "I didn't know that. She thinks you're supposed to deliver the ransom money?"

"That's what she said. Before she talked to me, the nice policeman in the baby's room asked me to do something important tonight, but he said he couldn't tell me what it was 'til later. I think he's goin' to tell me the same thing."

"Then it must be true. How did Miss Celly know?"

Danny shook his head. "I don't know. That made me think that Miss Celly took the baby. You helped me think that, too."

"I did?" she asked, her eyebrows raised. "How?"

He managed a smile. "You're nice to me, and you don't ask me for money. Every time Miss Celly is nice to me she asks me for money, but she was mean to me before I got my job. When she gave me the goldfish last night, she was nice, but she didn't ask for money. After she left, I tried to think why. Then I thought that maybe she wants to steal the money that I'm supposed to carry in the sack."

"The ransom money," Elsa mused out loud.

Danny got to his feet. "I need to go to work now. Will you please tell the police?"

"Yes," she answered, standing. "Right away. But I know they'll want to talk with you, too."

"Do you think they can talk with me in the kitchen, then?" he asked anxiously, glancing toward the hall. "We can talk while I work."

"I'll ask—" Elsa didn't finish, for the man with the newspaper was beside them.

"Excuse me," he said politely, motioning for Danny to stay. "I'm Sergeant Banks with Scotland Yard. "Would you mind coming upstairs with me?"

"I have to go to work," Danny told him. "Mr. Harold needs me."

"I'll let your employer know where you are," the man assured him. He smiled and pointed to the stairs. "Shall we?"

Eileen opened her eyes and looked around. The big person was in bed making noises with its mouth, and the not-so-big person lay on the sofa. She snuggled closer to the still baby, but the baby wasn't warm any more, even when Eileen put her back against its side.

Inspector McNeely took the hotel stairs two at a time on his way to suite twenty-one. The door to the suite opened as he was raising his hand to knock. Sergeant Banks stood in the doorway, smiling.

"We've got good news, Inspector," he reported as he followed McNeely inside.

At the table sat David Adams looking anxious and worried. Across the table from him, looking just as anxious, sat a tall young lady with striking blue eyes, and Danny.

Violet gave a last rub to the dress shop window and stepped back to survey her work. The advertisement for seamstresses was due to come out in that day's *Chronicle*, and she wanted any applicants to realize that this was a special place.

She wondered where Elsa had gone off to. Had she found a clue to Eileen's disappearance? *Father, please bring back that child*, she prayed. *Give Sarah and David the strength to endure this trial.*

If only she could go to Sarah and comfort her. Had she been wrong to get so involved with the shop when her friend needed her? *Oh, Father, please let Sarah know that my prayers are with her constantly.*

The door opened with a tinkling of bells, and Jacob came out carrying two cups of steaming tea. "You haff worked too hard," he scolded. "Even the busy ant knows there is a time to rest."

"I know," she said, giving him a grateful smile as she accepted her cup of tea. "I'm not tired, though."

He looking closely at her face. "Are you sure?"

"I'm just thinking about my friends and their baby."

"Ah yes," he said sadly. "Such a terrible thing. Vould you like to go and see your friend in the country? I could conduct the interviews."

"Thank you anyway, but I have to see what sewing skills the applicants have. After we've hired the seamstresses, though, do you think. . .?"

"Of course. Stay the rest of the week. Your friend will be glad to see you. Not haffing to buy fabric has saved us time. This business vill be a success, Miss Violet."

She smiled at him. "And I'm so glad to be part of it."

Jacob grinned and tugged at his beard. "A big part of it. I thank God for the day you came into this shop." Taking a sip of tea, he turned and studied the front door.

"Is anything wrong?" asked Violet.

He nodded. "I belief it is time to hang that sign over the door, don't you?"


Julia found Sarah at the kitchen table, helping Agnes and Ginny prepare breakfast for the boarders. "What are you doing here?" Julia asked, giving Agnes a worried glance.

Sarah looked up from the crusts she was rolling out for pear tarts. "Keeping busy, Julia. Keeping my thoughts occupied."

"Can I help you?" she asked, walking over to the table.

"Find me something to do after the breakfast dishes are cleared up," Sarah answered. "This is going to be the longest day of my life, and if I think about what might happen, I'll go crazy!"

"Perhaps a doctor. . .?"

"To drug me and put me to bed?" Sarah wiped her cheek with the back of her hand, leaving a bit of white flour under her eye. "I'd rather stay busy, my friend." Giving Julia a weak smile she added, "If there's one thing I'm good at, it's cleaning houses."


"That's where she lives," Danny said to Inspector McNeely, pointing to a battered wood door. They stood with a group of uniformed policemen in the middle of April Street. The stench of waste was so overwhelming that McNeely tried to speak without drawing air into his mouth.

"Are you sure?" he asked the boy.

"Yes sir."

"All right." He beckoned to one of the policemen. "Take him back to Palmer House."

"But I can show her to you," Danny protested.

The inspector shook his head. He'd almost had to arrest David Adams to convince him to stay at the hotel, and now the boy wanted to take part in the action.

"You've been a big help already, Danny. We know what the woman looks like—she's been workin' in this part of town for years. But we didn't know where she lived. Now we do."

When Danny had left with the officer, McNeely stepped over a pile of rotting fish heads, walked to the door, and knocked. Danny had told him there was no back door to the tenement, so he'd sent a couple men to stand guard under the lone window.

Inside, Raymond lifted his head from the mattress and shook it, trying to make the pounding go away. By the time he realized someone was at the door, he was clearheaded enough to look out the corner of the window.

*Don't panic*, he told himself when he saw the uniformed policemen. *They're lookin' for Celly, not me. I'll tell 'em she's gone off with somebody else.* He went back to the mattress, picked up Celly's moth-eaten blanket, and threw it over the body in the corner.

His hand was on the doorknob when he looked down at his shirt. It was splattered with blood. In one quick motion, he stripped it off and tossed it into the corner.

"What can I do for you, Officer?" he said, opening the

door just wide enough to peer at the men on the stoop.

"Inspector McNeely with Scotland Yard. We'd like to speak with Celly Tanner," said a man wearing a tweed frock coat.

"I'm sorry, sir, but she ain't here." His attempt to close the door was blocked by one of the policemen's nightsticks. "She took off with some other bloke," Raymond explained. "But I'll tell her you're lookin' for her if she comes back this way."

Inspector McNeely listened patiently. Putting a hand behind his back, he motioned for the officers standing behind him to come closer. "We'd like to come in and speak with you," he said.

"Uh, as you can see, I ain't exactly dressed for company," Raymond told him. "Why don't you come back later?" With his right hand and knee, he kept steady pressure against the door, but the officer with the nightstick wouldn't budge.

"I don't think we can do that. By the way, what's that on your face?"

"My face?" He touched his cheek with his left hand, then jerked his hand away and stared at the flakes of dried blood on his fingers. With a sigh, Raymond moved aside and made a courtly bow to the officers as they rushed in.

The old big person was up, moving around the shack. Eileen watched her, hoping the not-so-big person would get up soon and give her some water. Suddenly the big person came over to where she and the baby were. Making a loud noise with its mouth, the old big person bent down and picked up the baby. More noises came out of the old big person's mouth, and the not-so-big person came over and began to make loud noises too.

"Your child's kidnapper is dead," Inspector McNeely said as soon as he walked in the sitting room of the Adams's hotel suite. "But her murderer knows where the baby is. Would you like to come with us to fetch her?"

David's knees almost buckled as relief flooded through him. "Thank God!" he exclaimed, taking off into the bedroom to grab his riding boots. "Let's go now!"

Elsa threw open the door and rushed into the shop.

"Whatever is the matter?" Violet asked, looking up from a note she'd been reading.

"Eileen! The police are goin' to get her right now!"

"Oh, thank You, Lord!"

Elsa's tear-streaked face was all smiles as she embraced her friend. "You were right about us needing to have faith. He did answer our prayers, didn't He!"

"Yes, He sure did!" Wiping her eyes with her hand, Violet said, "What wonderful news!"

"You know how you said that maybe God sent me that dream about the person in black to jar my rememberin'?" Elsa asked, bubbling. "Well, that started it all." She looked down at the piece of paper in Violet's hand. "What's that you got there? It looks like a letter."

Violet quickly folded it and slipped it in her apron pocket. "It's nothing. Deborah brought something for me to read a little while ago."

"A secret?"

"Never mind," said Violet, gently pushing Elsa toward the door and ignoring her protests. "I'm expecting more people to come any minute and apply for the seamstress jobs, so why don't you run back to the hotel and keep an eye open? I want to know the minute that baby gets back."

When she was sure Elsa was gone, Violet took the note from her pocket and unfolded it. Smiling, she read the contents again.

> *Dear Miss Bowman,*
>
> *I asked Mrs. Turnley to take this to you, since she works near your dress shop. We are still praying for your friends and hope you will soon have good news to tell us at church.*
>
> *I have been told that Kennison Park is pleasant for picnicking on Sunday afternoons. Musicians are often there, and the fountain is beautiful. Would you mind having a picnic with me in the park after the service next week? Your friend Miss Stubbs is welcome to come, too.*
> *Sincerely,*
> *Luke Preston*

When she'd finished rereading the letter, Violet folded it back up and slipped it into her pocket. Walking over to the window, she looked out at the shops lining Redcliffe Street.

*Lord, thank You so much for answering our prayers about Eileen. And for making my sanctuary so much more than I dreamed it would be.* She was about to go back to work when she added, *And if Elsa's still living with me by this Sunday, please help her understand when I tell her she's got to walk home from church by herself.*

There wasn't enough water in the pail for Eileen to put

her face in and get a drink. After dipping her hand in and licking the drops from her fingers several times, she figured out that she could cup her hand and get more water.

A noise outside the door caught her attention. Though she was afraid of the old big person, Eileen hoped it and the not-so-big-person were back with the baby. She didn't like being left alone—even the little creatures with the long tails seemed to know that it was okay to scramble by and frighten her.

The door creaked open. Eileen shrank into the stones of the fireplace as the new big person walked in. It wasn't carrying a sack on its back, but it had the same smile that made her shudder.

"Well, whut do we have here?" it was saying as it walked closer. "Such a pretty little girl, and she ain't got nobody to play with."

It stopped. Cocking its head, it seemed to be listening. Seconds later Eileen heard rumbling, like the sound that the outside makes before water comes down. The new big person made an angry sound and ran outside.

"This is it," Raymond said as the horses hit a clearing in the forest.

David Adams jumped down from his horse and ran to the shack and through the open door with Inspector McNeely on his heels.

"Eileen!" he cried, holding out his arms and rushing to the fireplace, where the baby cowered beside a water bucket.

As her father scooped her up in his arms, Eileen buried her head in his neck and cried all the tears she'd had to hold back.

Sarah had the globes from the coal lamps in a pan of soapy water, handing them one at a time to Ginny to dry. "Do you remember when we had to do this every—"

"Sarah?"

Slinging water on the front of her dress, she turned. At the foot of the kitchen stairs stood her husband and baby.

"Eileen!" Sarah cried, running to take her in her arms. "My baby!"

Eileen latched on to her mother's neck as if afraid to let go, and David wrapped his arms around both of them. "She's all right," he said softly. "Our little girl's all right."

"You brought her back to me!" Sarah said through her sobs. "She's here, and I love you both so much!"

"God worked it out," David whispered. "It's incredible. We wouldn't have found her otherwise."

The kitchen was suddenly full with Julia, Agnes and Ginny, several policemen, and some of the boarders who had heard the excitement. David finally stepped back a bit from his wife and child so that the others could fuss over Eileen and share in the joy.

Later, when the freshly-bathed girl had fallen asleep in her mother's arms, Sarah laid her gently in the middle of her bed.

"Julia may have a crib," whispered David as he watched. "You aren't worried about her falling off the bed?"

Sarah smiled. "I'd like to sit and watch her sleep, if you don't mind. We can ask about a crib later."

Returning her smile, David walked over to the window and grabbed two wooden chairs. "We'll both watch her."

Two weeks later, Danny was sweeping the street outside

Palmer House Inn when he saw a familiar face coming toward him. "Elsa?"

The girl grinned, put a hand to her bonnet, and ran the last few feet. "I thought we'd never come back to town!" she chattered. "They're all at the grand opening of Violet's shop, but I couldn't wait to see the hero of Bristol!"

Blushing, he held aside his broom and shook her hand. "You're a hero, too. Miss Abby read me the stories in the newspaper about us."

"Miss Sarah cut them out," said Elsa. "She's gonna make me a scrapbook!"

"Can I see the baby sometime?"

"They're gonna be here in a little while. Miss Sarah ain't really met you, aside from seein' you outside the window."

Danny looked happy to hear this. "Mr. Adams came by one day with that nice policeman and gave me a lot of money. I told him he didn't have to do that, but he said he wanted me to have it."

"He did the same for me," said Elsa. "I've already invested mine in a certain dress shop. What are you gonna do with your hundred pounds?"

"Mr. Harold helped me put a lot of it in the bank to save. But I bought two new shirts and a bigger bowl for my goldfish."

"I forgot about your goldfish. Do they have names?"

Smiling, Danny said, "Elsa and Eileen."

# *A Letter To Our Readers*

Dear Reader:

In order that we might better contribute to your reading enjoyment, we would appreciate your taking a few minutes to respond to the following questions. When completed, please return to the following:

Karen Carroll, Editor
Heartsong Presents
P.O. Box 719
Uhrichsville, Ohio 44683

1. Did you enjoy reading *Shores of Deliverance*?
   ☐ Very much. I would like to see more books by this author!
   ☐ Moderately
      I would have enjoyed it more if _____

   _____

2. Are you a member of *Heartsong Presents*? Yes   No
   If no, where did you purchase this book? _____

   _____

3. What influenced your decision to purchase
   this book? (Circle those that apply.)

   | Cover | Back cover copy |
   |-------|-----------------|
   | Title | Friends |
   | Publicity | Other _____ |

4. On a scale from 1 (poor) to 10 (superior), please rate
   the following elements.

   ___Heroine        ___Plot

   ___Hero           ___Inspirational theme

   ___Setting        ___Secondary characters

5. What settings would you like to see covered in
   *Heartsong Presents* books?

   _____

   _____

6. What are some inspirational themes you would like
   to see treated in future books?_____

   _____

   _____

7. Would you be interested in reading other *Heartsong
   Presents* titles?               Yes       No

8. Please circle your age range:
   Under 18          18-24              25-34
   35-45             46-55              Over 55

9. How many hours per week do you read? _____

Name _____

Occupation _____

Address _____

City _____ State _____ Zip _____

add a little *MYSTERY*
to your romance!

## TWO GREAT INSPIRATIONAL ROMANCES
## WITH JUST A TOUCH OF MYSTERY
### *BY MARLENE J. CHASE*

_____*The Other Side of Silence*—Anna Durham finds a purpose for living in the eyes of a needy child and a reason to love in the eyes of a lonely physician...but first the silence of secrets must be broken. HP6 BHSB-07 $2.95.

_____*This Trembling Cup*—A respite on a plush Wisconsin resort may just be the thing for Angie Carlson's burn-out—or just the beginning of a devious plot unraveling and the promise of love. HP5 BHSB-05 $2.95.

# Inspirational Romance at its Best from one of America's Favorite Authors!

## FOUR HISTORICAL ROMANCES
### *BY COLLEEN L REECE*

___ *A Torch for Trinity*—When Trinity Mason sacrifices her teaching ambitions for a one-room school, her life—and Will Thatcher's—will never be the same. HP1 BHSB-01 $2.95

___ *Candleshine*-A sequel to *A Torch for Trinity*—With the onslaught of World War II, Candleshine Thatcher dedicates her life to nursing, and then her heart to a brave Marine lieutenant. HP7 BHSB-06 $2.95

___ *Wildflower Harvest*—Ivy Ann and Laurel were often mistaken for each other...was it too late to tell one man the truth? HP2 BHSB-02 $2.95

___ *Desert Rose*-A sequel to *Wildflower Harvest*—When Rose Birchfield falls in love with one of Michael's letters, and then with a cowboy named Mike, no one is more confused than Rose herself. HP8 BHSB-08 $2.95

# LOVE A GREAT LOVE STORY?

*Introducing Heartsong Presents —*
*Your Inspirational Book Club*

Heartsong Presents Christian romance reader's service will provide you with four never before published romance titles every month! In fact, your books will be mailed to you at the same time advance copies are sent to book reviewers. You'll preview each of these new and unabridged books before they are released to the general public.

These books are filled with the kind of stories you have been longing for—stories of courtship, chivalry, honor, and virtue. Strong characters and riveting plot lines will make you want to read on and on. Romance is not dead, and each of these romantic tales will remind you that Christian faith is still the vital ingredient in an intimate relationship filled with true love and honest devotion.

Sign up today to receive your first set. Send no money now. We'll bill you only $9.97 post-paid with your shipment. Then every month you'll automatically receive the latest four "hot off the press" titles for the same low post-paid price of $9.97. That's a savings of 50% off the $4.95 cover price. When you consider the exaggerated shipping charges of other book clubs, your savings are even greater!

**THERE IS NO RISK**—you may cancel at any time without obligation. And if you aren't completely satisfied with any selection, return it for an immediate refund.

**TO JOIN**, just complete the coupon below, mail it today, and get ready for hours of wholesome entertainment.

Now you can curl up, relax, and enjoy some great reading full of the warmhearted spirit of romance.

┌ ─ ─ ─ **Curl up with Heartsong!** ─ ─ ─ ┐

# YES! Sign me up for Heartsong!

**NEW MEMBERSHIPS WILL BE SHIPPED IMMEDIATELY!**
Send no money now. We'll bill you only $9.97 post-paid with your first shipment of four books. Or for faster action, call toll free 1-800-847-8270.

NAME _____

ADDRESS _____

CITY _____ STATE / ZIP _____

MAIL TO: HEARTSONG / P.O. Box 719 Uhrichsville, Ohio 44683

YES II